# HERO or VILLAIN

## Jim Williams

*Jason,*
*complete a small manuscript &*
*feel good, then think big; follow*
*your imagination.*
*Jim Williams*

*Man is evil - Genesis 3:22*

**Outskirts Press, Inc.**
**Denver, Colorado**

Hero or Villain

Outskirts Press, Inc.
http://www.outskirtspress.com

ISBN: 978-1-4327-2602-7

Library of Congress Control Number: 2008933551

Outskirts Press and the "OP" logo are trademarks belonging to Outskirts Press, Inc.

PRINTED IN THE UNITED STATES OF AMERICA

Hero
...one step at a time, climbing into his past...




Villain
...silent, animal rage erupting...

*The most difficult war we face is within ourselves.*
*- The author*

*I teach that all men are mad.*
*- Horace*

*Man is a rationalizing animal, not a rational animal.*
*- Aranson - psychologist*

*Forbidden knowledge is like a magnet;*
*drawing us in like the irresistible whisper.*
*- The author*

*Hero or Villain…based on a true story…*
July 18, 1984, a horrible event took place in McDonalds
in the San Ysidro section of San Diego, California.

# Acknowledgement

Profound thanks to my most creative friends Ivan Lozada and Richard Henning for their invaluable comments and advice.

Thanks to Lori Owens and Eduardo Sobenes for inspiration out of the box including the music of Hero Or Villain.

And many thanks to friends who inspired my creativity and spurred me on to finish my first novel, Hero Or Villain. Thanks to those who showed incredible support and who asked to preview the draft version; you made the moment of having my first literary baby my most thrilling.

# 1993

Another year of global oddities, including UFO abductions in Australia. Most were devoid of physical evidence; however, the 1993 Narre Warren incident is one of the few compelling exceptions. Here, we are dealing with an event that appears to involve physical evidence and three groups of apparently independent witnesses who may confirm a disquieting reality.

In 1994, Chicago, Illinois, according to his wife, Neil Petterson disappeared for two months when he drove north toward Lake Michigan. She came home one day and found him sleeping in their bed. His face was dark with a severe tan. He was Caucasian and had trouble tanning at the pool. His body was pale. When he woke, he related a bizarre story over and over. "They probed my mind incessantly, allowing little sleep. They asked why humans were cruel to each other. I told them I didn't know the reason." His therapist said he probably would never be the same.

UFO experts assert from victim accounts that abductions involve extensive efforts by aliens - for whatever purpose - to understand the human psyche.

For those on earth intently involved in the study of humans, all psychology journals come to the same conclusion: The human psyche will probably remain a mystery.

# Prologue

*Does madness run in my family?*

*Climbing the attic ladder, Julian Barrin obsessed about Professor Dawson's assessment of mankind. 'Man is evil!'*

*Am I going mad? The sinister doubt had a genetic link and had become a 10-year obsession. And now Dawson had added fuel to the inferno.*

*And a journal in a family locker surely was proof of Julian's destiny.*

*An ancestor had committed a brutal act of murder using bizarre creative methods. Another ancestor had chronicled the event, leaving the evidence in a locker for Julian to discover. The locker was an unwitting time machine containing bizarre news that others would have burned or buried.*

*The psych professor shared horrifying facts with the class about the cruelties that man is capable of. "Ted Bundy was a cult classic hero for many warped souls." FBI files contain the best horror novels. Truth is stranger than fiction. Authors could never come up with the deep dark horror that the evil man is capable of. Never.*

*Desire is real.*

*Fiction is a stretch of imagination. Imagination has boundaries.*

*Desire is boundless.*

*Fiction can never stretch to the point of the evil desire a*

Bundy can reach. Evil reality is a playful bomb going off in Bundy's hungry synapses. It becomes an addiction. Ergo, serial killers with an insatiable taste for someone else's blood.

The musty smell wafted down to the form on the ladder and the dusty pungent aroma of pine and attic mites kicked up his sinuses. At the top of the stairs, Julian thought about the shocking discovery he had made 10 years ago in the dusty old family locker that waited. The genetic link alluded to. Julian had choked on the words that forewarned him of his heritage.

He was certain that the locker was possessed. Possession was his only hope.

His fate was at the mercy of the locker. And the voices of his ancestors. Julian thought with bitter irony, If I ever mentioned this to Professor Dawson he would use me as an example in future classes.

Madness was man's destiny if born to the wrong genes. After reading the shocking news in the old journal, Julian had joined the university Psychology 101 class to gain knowledge about the human psyche to understand and instill confidence in his own mental health. Instead of assurance, Julian was mortified of the possibility that genetics damned him to a life not so different from Bundy. Waiting for him along with the mites and musty molecules living in the stale and possessed air of the attic were shocking facts about a cousin who had died in an asylum and apparently was treated as another Ted Bundy ahead of his time.

Julian had to find out if he was destined to be tortured by shock therapy in an asylum.

Jekyll and Hyde personalities could be in battle in his mind without his knowledge.

He suddenly felt light headed and then...

"It's okay."

It should have been reassuring but he didn't know if it was his own delusion acting up. His own mind game. Or whispers from the ghosts in the shadows above?

He thought about Einstein and how much the genius must have enjoyed his own thoughts.

He soberly thought about his own mind. The mind is not a Disney World joy ride; it's a rat's maze.

Was someone from his past trying to reach him? Or was it

*his imagination...was he really going...mad?*

*He remembered the cliché: The truth shall set you free.*

*Maybe I don't really want to know. Maybe the truth will shackle me to a tormented future!*

*Like the flame attracts the moth, the ancestral secrets within the locker in the attic attracted Julian Barrin.*

*For nearly ten years, Julian had the same thought. He wished to God he'd never found the damn thing.*
**1993**

# CHAPTER 1

**P**ulling on the rope, the anticipation was as strong as the last time, exactly one year ago. The doubt was even stronger. The ghostly whispers becoming louder. Today was his 10-year anniversary for this ritual. For 10 years Julian's crusade was never jubilant, it was rather...a toil. But he was motivated to keep trying. Answers could be waiting. Something he had missed might rise from the past. The mind can be scary if you don't know whether you're destined to go insane.

Maybe the whole thing, the voices promising truth, has been a figment of my imagination. Wishful thinking, like Christmas.

10 years and he recently added a new twist to his journey. A class in psychology to better understand the mind. His mind. Professor Dawson didn't exactly enlighten him during the first class telling everyone how vague psychology really is. Not an exact science. 10 years is nothing, he had said, when dealing with the mind. Some shrinks spend 15 years with the same patient to have successfully dealt with only one of the patient's phobias. He had quit smoking. However, he related that he still had strong urges driving down the freeway. The thought of what it would feel like to shoot a hitchhiker while he sped by. The dark side was still dark.

And sometimes the dark memory needs a rest.

*It takes many strange things to bring the traumatized memory to the surface at times.* Professor Dawson.

Impropriety was waiting in Julian's future. A violent family faux paux he wished he had never been privy to had twisted his reality to the point of breaking.

Julian placed his right foot on the first rung preparing to climb to the haunted attic and, like a canoe in unchartered swirling water, carefully drift through the cerebral fog to the locker in a tight corner where a journal of frightening innuendos waited. Where he would attempt to face his genetic phobias. But so far, no answers. *Why do you keep calling me? Why do I keep coming? You only disappoint me time after time. Is this what haunting and possession are all about? Perhaps I should bring Professor Dawson with me. Now there's a field trip for you. Humor mixed with madness.*

Today Julian was facing his phobias, his dark side - if there was one.

Oh there is a dark side, you can count on that, Professor Dawson concurred. Man is evil. Genesis.

We know the truth about Santa Claus, yet every year we hand little kids an icon, a doll, of the fat man, and we place the Star of David on top of the tree. A ritual with a different ghost.

Looking up at the opening he just created in the attic floor, Julian's heart pounded. Why did it pound so hard? He was no stranger to what waited above in the attic.

Perhaps this has been 10 years of illusion. The voices, those faint whispers, seem real when I open the locker and I'm digging into my ancestor's past.

He squeezed the frail wooden railing and shook it, thinking, If I hadn't found the locker and that journal I would be blissfully ignorant.

Julian was torn between ecstasy and dread as he climbed the drop-down stairs, climbing into his past, holding onto the wooden slats at the side, one step at a time, the steps feeble under foot, but not dangerous. Finally at the top, his hands grabbed for a secure hold on the familiar, vertical two-by-four. He paused to listen for anything extraordinary. He heard only his exasperation. His labored breathing. *What did you expect?*

Grabbing overhead support, he angled his body and stepped over the framework where the steps would fold up later when he finished. He carefully monkey walked along ceiling struts to his destination, a corner lighted softly by the tiny front window and the air vent.

As he closed in on the locker, he flicked aside Christmas tree ornaments that brushed his forehead, and he laughed out loud at himself. At the audacity of the ritual – 10 years! And his imagination...*I'm not alone up here*. And it's not Santa Claus waiting.

Taking a deep breath, he tried not to hurry. Special occasions like this were supposed to have an element of serenity. His *friends* could wait. The ghosts. They had waited this long.

Apparently the early sun shifted... there was Shadow Play... Don't play with me...my own mind has that luxury.

Another shift...Shadow Play...The attic was alive with...life...it would seem...*doppelgangers, perhaps*...at that whimsical thought, Julian laughed again, a nervous laugh, then held his breath; his senses on full alert as he stepped to yet another attic strut, careful not to fall. After all, he didn't want to be the butt of jokes for a bunch of ghosts.

And yet another shift, a skeleton danced in the corner of his bearing in the shaft of light. Not a skeleton, tree branches.

He glanced at his watch and grimaced. He wasn't giving himself as much time as the previous years. He was giving too much credit to those inhabitants that weren't real. Or, maybe it was because he was finally tired of the whole thing. Maybe his past and his phobias were starting to bore him. Or scare him. *Patience!* Did I think that? Or... Okay! I hear you! He looked at the corner in the attic and the locker that waited. He smiled in spite of the fear that began rolling down his cheeks in sweat beads.

How odd. It was cold and he was sweating.

And for the first time, he had real expectations. Probably because of the accident, the strong feeling of loss – of the many losses over the years that were now taking their toll. His whole family was somehow with him this morning, some strolling in this attic, some loitering in the locker...so he had a right to expectations. The mind must have its pleasure whether fanciful or fearful...he looked about...the locker was closer. And he actually smirked whether the ghosts liked it or not...he damn well had a right to a whimsical moment after 10 years of fear of his family and his own psyche. He made his way to the corner in the attic where a shaft of light bled through, and his dark side crouched in front of the dusty old time machine, the locker, leaving the light peeking over his shoulders.

# CHAPTER 2

**Little Rock, Arkansas**

On the day of the presidential inauguration, an unusual ritual was being performed at 3721 Roosevelt Drive in a northeastern suburb of the President's hometown.

Julian Barrin crouched in front of an old locker placed decades ago in the dusty attic possibly by his grandparents, but definitely by someone who wanted to keep the locker and its contents from prying eyes. The contents were not conversation pieces, unless one whispered them.

This was why the locker did not reside in the den, but remained in the attic.

Since they didn't bring it up, out of respect and maybe a little fear, he never talked with his parents about the locker. Fear of what, he wasn't certain, but he surmised that it was fear of...the truth. Family phobias.

He discovered the locker by accident ten years ago today while rummaging around for a Halloween costume. That day he had spent two hours sifting through his family's past, and there it was. An unexpected connection to his ancestors. *Why me? Before the discovery, blissful ignorance, and he wasn't creeping about in some dusty attic listening for people who weren't there.*

For ten years Julian had struggled to understand the essence of a journal he stumbled onto by accident in the attic. He hoped the struggle was nearing its end and that the truth would indeed set him free. The journal contained frightening violent facts and innuendoes. Warnings making him guilty by genetic association. An ancestor had made headlines. He had inherited genes that would make him like the larvae and the butterfly. Only his change might not be so delightful as a butterfly. His change might cause horses to rear and dogs to bark out of fear of what their sixth sense warned them. *A monster approaches.*

"Okay, I'm here."

And now, he was about to perform the same ritual he had for ten years since discovering the chest and its contents. It was Friday morning, January 20, 1993, in Little Rock, Arkansas. And as usual, he felt he was about to learn something new about his past, maybe something redeeming. But like watching a movie with a bad ending for the tenth time, he figured that part would be the usual disappointment, no change. The plot was frozen, and, he figured, so was his life.

"According to Professor Dawson, I brought my dark side with me. Can you help me? *Help us?*"

Silence. What the hell did he expect? With a wry smile, he grunted. The attic was a claustrophobic world. Sound fell to the earth like a crippled thing. Up here in this insulated environment, his voice fell on deaf ears. Or did it?

He was never certain why, but he always felt like a thief, like the raccoon, or the crow that searches for something to plunder, then leaves nothing of value in its place. The only thing he would leave today was his fingerprint.

Squatting over the chest, and with his blond hair in attractive disarray around his head and shoulders, his soft blues eyes were eager and alert as though this were the first exploration of the old chest. Delicate, long fingers lifted the metal clasp, raised the heavy wooden lid with a creak. He felt expectations rising, as though he would discover something new this time – *something redeeming.*

"Time for discovery," he told himself. "So, discover something, Sigmund Freud."

*Be careful what you ask for.* A breath. Ragged. Ghostly. Not his.

It was barely a whisper, barely reality...his imagination. And for the first time during these rituals, he felt there was more than one. One whispering. One observing. One breathing.

"Oh really," he said under his breath, just in case.

"I think I am amusing these ghosts." His admonishment was barely above a whisper, or even a thought. A statement of irony that was perhaps for the pleasure of the residents who might be hiding and snickering.

"Thank God you haven't been laughing, I will say that for you."

Julian's attitude had recently metamorphosed. Thanks in part to Professor Dawson's class. While he was tormented by the possibility that his destiny was to be his nightmare and a shrink's cerebral buffet, he also figured he had an emotional investment. His family, his own, and his tormentors' – the ghosts – and 10 years ago he would have been the one snickering about such a quaint thought. Ghosts. Until he discovered this damn time machine from his ancestors. And heard their voices. That was the part that alarmed him. *I'm either a medium or a madman.*

Julian's mind was full of raw emotion and his imagination was a kaleidoscope of images! Too many coincidences. Two sets of twins, same names, one definitely mad, a murderer long ago. The other set of twins today, and perhaps one definitely going mad while hanging around in the attic possessed by ancestor ghosts. Man is evil! And death doesn't always kill the evil in man.

*That is a scary thought up here alone with all these ghosts!*

Julian peered inside, into the dusty past. He smelled the familiar scent of the contents, the dust, the documents, and miscellaneous artifacts from his ancestor's past. Sunlight squeezed through slats of an air vent in the eve of his late parents old two-story frame house, the light between the sharp, rapier shadows, revealed chapters from the past whose strange dark reality eluded him, and within their mysterious pages. . .knowledge awaited him, waiting to be read. But was there something to learn, something he always missed while sifting through this antiquated locker from his past?

"What am I really after?" he quietly asked himself for the hundredth time while poking at the objects carefully placed in the same position after each reading. Peace. The answer hadn't changed since the first reading, the first time he had learned something he wished to God he had never discovered. He was after...peace, peace of mind.

As he squatted down in this familiar place, he thought about peace. Would something inside this dusty time machine, something foreboding but enlightening, which continued to elude his search year after year, give him that peace? Would that something tell him that he was... That he was what? That he was okay? He smiled at himself and his embarrassing innocence.

Is the whole family really this bonkers? He shook his head. I really tire of this.

Julian focused on the object of his ritual, the item that demanded his attention year after year. A family journal encrusted in once polished leather that was now time worn, an uneven dark brown, and musty smelling.

But something was wrong.

He paused in his effort to explore and considered the inside of the locker -- the objects. He always left things in a certain order. Somehow that order had been disturbed. He couldn't quite put his finger on it, but...he could sense it.

Maybe his parents...no, he shook his head at the thought. They were too old to be venturing up here, climbing up those feeble steps. Whatever the reason, whoever the culprit, he wouldn't let the impertinent behavior ruin this moment. He set aside the knowledge that his sacred sanctity had been disturbed and moved on with the ritual.

Julian's blue eyes suddenly revealed the sadness that was always inevitable when he saw the aged journal and the joy of anticipation left him. Lying inside was a time-yellowed parchment, a diary, containing family secrets. Each reading caused more obsessions with the psyche...the human mind...and more concern for his own mind. Because of this audacious annual event, his heritage haunted him. The dark side. Every family has a dark side! Man is evil. Professor Dawson. Perhaps the Professor is in cahoots with you guys! He smiled at his ignorant brilliance. Ignorance is bliss. Julian knew he could stop this obsession. He also knew he didn't want to.

The journal's terrifying revelations and Professor Dawson's inspirations triggered new levels of fear rather than solace of knowledge. Now his imagination terrified him because he imagined the worst...that his dark side was an animal tearing at the chains that restrained him and that those restraints were failing. And the same terror rose like bile in the pit of his stomach – fear for what heredity did to his own sanity.

Turning to the next page his head shot forward and his eyes widened in horror and disbelief. The page! The intrusion had manifested itself. A blatant impropriety! An act of undue intimacy in his private world to be exact! "What the hell?" He gasped with indignation.

He looked up, stared straight ahead into the shadows expecting mocking laughter. Then Julian whirled around in his claustrophobic sanctity, carefully scanning all peripherals of the attic, but all shadows with their backs to him were still. Though he felt a presence, none were breathing. None stared back. He shuddered and caught his breath.

"I am crazy!" He cried out in a raspy whisper.

His eyes shot back to the page and, nostrils flaring, he gritted his teeth. Did I do this? Or did they make me do this and taunt me with it? The perfect page he had looked at one year ago, that he had turned like any other page, today had flipped out of its binder. The once-perfect page contained the most incriminating evidence that his ancestors were insane. And that perhaps he too would wake up one morning and feel like someone else and perhaps go hunting on the freeway. The names were as terrifying as the horrible acts of murder. They were too coincidental. Who was playing with family history? Not only did his family seem loco, but loco by design. Someone from years ago seemed to understand genetic inheritance when they named this baby. He straightened the page enough to read the words.

*January 20, 1920. My name is Kevin Barrin. Yesterday morning my parents were found dead. Their throats slit. In lieu of being hanged, my twin brother, their seventeen-year-old son, Julian, will be sent to an asylum.*

*To think they gave him so much love and that was how he*

*repaid them. He was always acting weird; putting bugs in the soup when mother was cooking dinner. Or snakes in their beds.*

Trying to regain his composure. Everything was spinning out of control. Genetics and recent visits by someone.

Someone had been here and desecrated his sanctuary! He inhaled a deep, ragged breath, indignation and anger building beyond comprehension.

Someone had ripped the page away from the wire retainer and then crudely shoved it back in where it would never again look like it belonged.

Someone had been here within the past year.

Julian was crazy with resentment. He wasn't breathing and he finally gasped, *"What the-*Who the hell?!" He never imagined another human being standing in his sacred spot.

He couldn't focus.

Ten years and he still shuddered when he read the names. The twins' names.

"Who in the world?" he wondered in amazement trying to let go of his anger.

The page was wrinkled indicating that whoever had been here had ripped the page away from the binder in a rage.

Maybe his parents...but why? He would never know, so he tried to dismiss it. Nothing would be gained by being upset. But he *was* upset. Someone had been here.

*So what?* Somewhere, an indignant whisper.

*It's okay.*

"Am I imagining this?" He looked around the attic for any clue. Another shift. More shadow play. "Are you real?"

*Is it my dark side fooling me or your humor trying to amuse me?*

"So you're still here," Julian thought aloud in ironic amusement, anger still smoldering. "So maybe you saw, maybe you know," he said in an accusing and imploring tone, but not expecting any help. He took a deep breath. "And maybe to hell with you," he said, and exhaled.

In the cold attic, Julian's breath shrouded the page like a fog. He squeezed his hands to aid circulation; the humidity and low temperature caused a biting frost. The cold chilled his indignation and angry thoughts, which subsided for the moment, and he continued reading.

*Yesterday, everyone showed sympathy. But today, the shock has mostly worn off, and they're starting to look at me strange. Like maybe I had something to do with it. I even heard Mrs. Martin whispering to one of her friends "It runs in the family, you know. They're twins and twins are more alike than we can imagine. They're all just alike, blond headed and blue eyed."*

*Signed: Kevin Barrin.*

There was an old, black and white photo, still clear, its borders jagged, as were photos of that time, adding a sinister effect. Julian was tall, the blond hair looking dirty white, and those dark, threatening blue eyes. The picture of Kevin was identical. He too was tall; however, his eyes were a friendly, lively dark.

While he rummaged in the past looking for more clues that might alleviate his paranoia about his genetic prophecy, Julian thought about his own brother. A brother he hardly knew. His parents had told him very little about Kevin. That he had died while they were both less than a year old. He was Julian's twin.

Julian's memories didn't match what his parents told him. He thought he could remember having a brother at age three, and then suddenly a world without a brother. Like the brother had been only a dream. A strange incoherent memory.

Perhaps this went along with his phobia about his psyche.

Compounded by an attic that seemed haunted by dancing ghosts and ancestors hiding in a locker along with voices and letters and pictures with jagged edges.

Perhaps there was evidence.

That he really was crazy like his ancestors.

Enough of these thoughts.

There was more, about his family, recently deceased, removed from his world because of a horrible accident, but the usual enchanting spell created by the attraction of his ancestor's ancient mental disorder recorded and left behind in the attic was broken by an unknown intruder. Julian considered cutting the ritual short, putting the journal back in the locker, closing the lid. Every time he read the journal he felt guilt, by association, he figured. Julian and Kevin were cousins he never met. But to have a cousin who was known, or at least, thought to be, *insane*. Heredity was scary. Those chromosomes, genes, and all. Like a dark side that might exist due to something out of your control.

He became aware of eyes peering at him. His own. He looked in a tall, oval mirror standing behind the locker. The resemblance was there, he couldn't deny it. Tall, blond, blue eyed.

But sane, he quickly assured himself.

Time to go. Did you hear me?

With a flourish, he put everything back just the way he found it for whatever good it would do now. Would he be back next year? Someone had invaded his world, robbed him of his privacy. It did not matter that the person was family or not. His sanctity was marred by intrusion.

*You'll be back. You need...us.*

The voice was faint, but distinguishable. Don't be so sure of yourself.

"My imagination scares me sometimes," said Julian, just to hear a real voice.

Time for closure. He reached for the heavy lid to put an end to this visit. His emotions were seething. He slowly moved the lid through its arc to shut out his past. Without warning his hand shot back inside the locker, grabbing the journal that had been desecrated by someone. "I implore you! Cousins! AM I going mad?" Another shift by the sun in the far corner. The skeleton danced again. "Do you mock me?" The heavy tree branches swept the eve of the old house making a moaning sound. He raised the journal to his head, closed his eyes. Listened. Am I? The journal was the last link to his ancestors. One who had gone mad. The pages, including the desecrated page, were a testament that his lineage was in torment. The mind was indeed fragile. His psych professor – Professor Dawson - had made this clear. *This frontier will remain a mystery.*

Julian opened his eyes and carefully placed the journal back where it had rested for decades.

He closed the lid carefully and it snapped shut with a solid click.

His fingers swept over the length of the locker, like rubbing a magic lantern. *I just wanted validation.*

He glanced resentfully at the corner where the last shift had occurred; shadow play and the dancing skeleton. *All you gave me was your usual taciturn.*

Julian looked at his watch. 7:45AM

Nothing redeeming today, he thought, closing the lid.

"Big help you guys are."

No response. No whispers. No validation.

Julian headed downstairs from the attic leaving behind his taciturn ancestors. He folded the stairs back into their lofty wood-framed bed in the ceiling. His sacred solitude was sealed again, but obviously not protected from prying eyes or ill-conceived acts. He looked around the room, the house, and up at the ceiling hiding the recessed ladder with the rope hanging down, inviting someone to pull it. Someone indeed had. He shook his head at the sheer audacity, the impudent act of the intrusion.

He turned and looked at the front door, and wondered, Who was the intruder? And he thought about the journal and the name, Kevin. His dead twin who suddenly disappeared was Kevin. Was everyone aware of that, or just Julian? Did someone decide to honor Kevin the ghost giving his name to Julian's late twin? So many eerie thoughts.

"Until next year," he proclaimed, and mentally saluted the attic and the locker. And, then, imagining the physical act of someone entering the house, and, with malice opening the attic door with deliberate thoughts of invading Julian's privacy, he promised, "I'll deal with the reality another time." This was how psychologists advised people to deal with their issues. Confront them!

He had enough time to stop at McDonald's, have breakfast, and head for classes. He was majoring in psychology. He had an obsession with the workings of the mind. He realized his obsession was driven by his own fear of what his psyche, his own mind, could become. This reality came to fruition 10 years ago when he started hearing voices upon reading that he might be crazy thanks to his ancestors. Thanks to the revelations held inside a locker in the attic. He was confronting his ghosts. A healthy attitude. He smiled. Then he stopped short just as he touched the doorknob.

The big question. Was his fear of learning the truth about his own mind justified?

Only his friends knew the answer. And they were tucked away in the locker. And today, they weren't talking.

# CHAPTER 3

"**C**an I help you?" asked the pert young waitress behind the counter.

"I'll have the McMuffin special."

On the counter, next to the waitress, sat a television monitor, placed there temporarily for patrons to witness Governor Bill Clinton's inaugural address to take place in just two hours in Washington, D. C.

Three minutes later Julian sat at a yellow plastic table in a yellow plastic chair in the dining room just around the corner from the counter.

Besides five animated youngsters in the restaurant, occupying a booth was a young woman sitting next to a man, possibly her boyfriend. There were also four men and three women, science majors, who went to the same college Julian attended just across the street; the University of Arkansas at Little Rock. Julian had never had an occasion to meet them. Very few people did know him.

Julian's contract with Westinghouse had ended, school was beginning, and he had moved back from Rhode Island to take over his parent's house. They were killed in a car wreck two months before. He decided going to school would be good to take his mind off his loss.

From his seat he could see the perimeter of the University and students walking to class. Behind the restaurant was an elementary school where the children were enrolled.

Julian chewed on a bite of the McMuffin sandwich, and took a drink of orange juice. He looked at his watch. 8:15. His class began at 8:30.

He leaned back for a second, took a deep breath, and considered the morning in the attic. He could not deny his anger or his curiosity about who had invaded his private world. He was certain it had not been his parents. They were not good at climbing those steps anymore. So who had been in the locker?

His reverie was interrupted when his peripheral vision detected motion, an involuntary action where the mind is a curious thing, curious about the unknown that enters its world.

A young man came through the front door, held onto it, turned, let go, and stared back at the parking lot as he backed toward the counter.

"Hey, watch where you're going!" yelled a ten-year-old, juice spilling on her tray.

There's one of my subjects now, thought Julian in amusement. I'll bet my friends in the attic would love to meet him.

The man's eyes were wild. People started shaking their heads.

Julian watched curiously. The man was blond headed, maybe Julian's age of twenty-three, tall, wearing a beard, and needing a haircut, or at least a brush. His clothes looked as though they had been slept in. He wore a black leather jacket.

He didn't head for the counter, but instead, walked to a booth and slid in. He stared out the window, toward the parking lot, as though he were waiting for someone.

Two ten-year old boys began chasing each other, one tripped over the newcomer's feet, jarring him in his seat. Again his eyes went wide. He looked down at the boy as though he were staring at an escaped animal from the zoo.

Another couple of kids came running around the booth,

jeering at the one who fell.

Julian shook his head at all the commotion that morning. Another glance at his watch. 8:20. He stood, headed for the trash container, pushed the flap open and banged the tray to remove all debris. He jumped at the noise; it was much louder than expected.

Someone screamed.

He turned to look apologetic and froze. Just around the corner he could see that the bearded man was holding a gun. The boy who had fallen to the floor had been shot. Blood was beginning to soak his shirt.

Without a word, the man suddenly opened fire, shooting everyone in sight – silent, animal rage erupting. Children were screaming. Those with the facility of mind sought cover. Too late. Without flinching, methodically, he reloaded with a fresh clip, ran around the corner and shot the three startled waitresses. One male student made a dash for the door but the killer fired, the bullet ripping through the man's neck and shattering the door. His body sprawled hideously across the now empty frame joining the myriad pieces of glass that had seconds before been a complete glass door.

Horrified, Julian watched, wide-eyed and breathless, from behind a trash container at the opposite end of the room. These were the people he intended to study. Now he had to figure out a way to survive the day with this kind of person.

Grabbing a tray, and breathing ever so quietly, he silently scooted toward the front, and crouched behind another trash container.

Holding the gun like a divining rod, the man came around the corner searching for more victims. Julian struck out with the tray. The action caught the gunman by surprise, knocking the gun from his hand after firing wildly, shattering a large window. The gun slid toward the door, jamming against the dead student's foot, while the gunman, thrown off balance, fell toward the counters.

Nearly in shock, and not aware he was even moving, Julian quickly ran and grabbed the .22-caliber pistol from the floor and jerked up ready to fire.

At the same instant, the gunman regained his balance and started toward Julian. A couple of quick monkey-like steps, and the man stopped right in front of his intended victim who stared for a split second at wild blue eyes filled with hysteria. Without pausing, the gunman whipped out a duplicate .22-caliber pistol.

Julian had no choice. He shot his would-be killer in the chest. Wild disbelief covered the gunman's face and his pistol went off a split second later.

Julian flinched, expecting to feel pain but the .22 had discharged into linoleum. Then the gunman slumped like a sack of potatoes to the floor.

Overwhelmed by his act of violence, and the hideous sight, breathing with jerky breaths, Julian stared down at the body. He had never shot anyone; had fired a gun only a few times.

The whole episode since the first shot had taken less than two minutes.

He looked around the restaurant. He was surrounded by a nightmare. Blood was everywhere. All the children, everyone, appeared to be dead. Wait. There was movement by one person. The young girl in the booth, her head lay on the table. He noticed she was holding her stomach, blood oozing from between her fingers.

Julian started toward her, trembling, still holding the gun.

Her head lifted, revealing dark brown hair matted around her forehead. She was very attractive even under these circumstances. Blue eyes widened with terror.

He paused. "Wait a minute. You think I shot you. It wasn't me," he explained, shaking his head. "It was him," he said, pointing toward the dead killer lying on the floor.

"You're bleeding. Can I help you?" he asked, his voice trembling.

Her eyes wide with fear, catatonic like, she turned her head and gazed at her boyfriend slumped over in the booth, then slowly she looked back to Julian, and finally, at the killer on the floor.

As much as he wanted, he dared not approach her just yet, possibly frighten her even more. He repeated, "Will you let me help you?"

The girl made no sign of understanding, her face only contorted with grimaces. He figured she was in too much pain and shock.

# CHAPTER 4

**H**is head jerked around. The noise was upon him suddenly; a squad of cars was approaching, their sirens shrieking mercilessly.

He looked at the girl who was still lying there, her face displaying desperation and fear. "Thank God! They're coming," said Julian, hoping to instill hope into the girl. She did not seem to hear him.

He started toward the door, walked carefully around the killer's and the victims' bodies, avoiding the pools of blood.

A parade of cars roared into view. Half a dozen squad cars veered into the parking lot, lights flashing, sirens screeching. Four officers jumped from their cars on the side opposite the restaurant, 45-caliber pistols drawn. They immediately saw the body in the door, and, seeing Julian standing there, gun in hand, they flipped their safeties off.

"This is the police, you are surrounded. Come out with your hands up."

Mouth agape, Julian's eyes went wide with fear and disbelief. He jumped back from the door. He looked at the gun in his hand and stared at the entourage swarming the parking lot and the truth hit him far too late. He was the hero. But to more than a dozen excited cops, he was the gun-wielding killer.

"We will give you no more warnings. Come out with your hands above your head."

Julian looked at the injured girl. She didn't seem aware that the police had arrived. She just stared back at Julian wide-eyed and then suddenly collapsed.

Outside, shaking his head in disbelief, an officer with binoculars was watching Julian. He could see pools of blood and a couple of bodies on the floor by the door.

"I didn't do it!" Julian yelled through the door. "I'm the one who stopped him."

"This is Lieutenant Brown. There's bodies lying around in there, Mister, and you're the one holding the gun," yelled the lieutenant.

Julian inched toward the door. "I did not shoot these people!" he declared frantically. "I'm a student, not a killer."

"What's your name, son?" asked Brown in a calmer voice.

"Julian Barrin."

"Where do you live, Julian?"

"3721 Roosevelt Drive. A house. By myself," he responded.

"Are you refusing to come out, Julian?" asked another cop, his gun poised for a shot at the front door.

"I just want to set the record straight before this thing gets out of hand," he replied. "There's a girl in here who's still alive. She's bleeding badly, and needs immediate attention. She can tell you I'm innocent."

The officers did not respond.

"No one shoots until I say," ordered Brown, eyeing the deputy whose eyes were sighting down his service revolver at the door. The man threw a begrudging smile at his superior officer.

"Yes, sir."

Brown reached inside his car and grabbed the microphone. "HQ, this is unit 7, we have a code blue."

"Did you hear me? There's a badly wounded girl in here," yelled Julian. He looked at the girl and shook his head, feeling helpless and thinking, Why the hell did this have to happen?

Anger struck at him for a brief moment and he looked down at the dead man who had just turned his life into a living hell. And it suddenly struck him that he didn't know the identity of the man he had shot and killed. The body was face down and he could see the outline of a wallet in the left pocket.

"Send all the ambulances available to the McDonald's restaurant on University." Brown took a deep breath. "Might as well send the ME. Unit 7 out."

"10-4, Unit 7, ambulances are on the way, along with the ME. HQ clear."

The noise came from the speakers mounted on top of the black and whites, along with a flood of uniforms, and a growing crowd of spectators lining the sidewalk along University Avenue, creating a circus-like atmosphere. But it was the beginning of a second nightmare for Julian.

The excitement was taking its toll on the sluggish hero. Julian was near shock realizing they really thought he was the one who shot these people. They would shoot him if he didn't surrender. But if he did surrender, how would he prove his innocence? He felt he had to make a stand; force the truth now.

He considered the irony of the situation. He was going to class. He was a student in psychology - not a killer. That was his cousin's deed. His cousin. Julian had a very deductive mind. His next thought caused his heart to pound. The locker and the diary. His heritage. His worst nightmare could become reality. He could be deemed insane, and, under the right circumstances, all hell could break loose and he was standing right in the middle of those circumstances.

Then he remembered a similar incident he had read about in a psychology book. The man in the tower in Austin, Texas, who shot numerous people - mostly students. "These guys probably remember that one too," he mumbled to himself.

In his imagination, everything was snowballing. His situation was getting more critical by the minutes. "Gotta keep a cool head, before I loose it - literally," he admonished himself.

Again,he looked at the outline of the wallet. He had a strong impulse to go over and remove it. But right now he had more problems than knowing the killer's name. He had to convince the men outside with guns that the dead man on the floor was the killer.

He looked back at the unconscious girl. She was his only witness, and she hadn't spoken a word since being shot.

He needed help.

His mind started again. He listened closely...but nothing was there. No Shadow Play. Not a whisper.

Don't you guys ever come out? I could sure use some help. Thought you guys had all the answers. I come to you every year. It's your turn. He shook his head and smiled at his momentary insanity. Crazy distractions sometimes help in extreme circumstances. But today wasn't his day. He grunted a hopeless laugh.

Nothing to laugh about, my friend.

His smile abruptly vanished. His thought, or someone else's?

No. He was back to square one with no one but himself to turn to.

# CHAPTER 5

*9:02AM McDonald's*

**M**ore sirens. A convoy of five ambulances, and a black car with ME on its side, roared into the parking lot. The ambulances backed in, parking parallel to the playground in front of McDonald's. The attendants crawled out as though exiting a helicopter, and hurried toward Lieutenant Brown's car.

"Julian, ambulance attendants and the ME are here. Will you let them come in and get the girl and the bodies?"

"Yes, but I do not intend to be taken to jail like a criminal. I haven't done anything wrong."

Julian could hear the Lieutenant giving instructions to the medics.

"Don't mess with this guy. He could be extremely dangerous. Just get the girl and the others and get out as quickly as possible." Ten medics nodded in agreement. They wanted no part of the violence. In synchronization, they threw open the rear doors, pulling out the stretchers.

The bystanders, gaping, were watching, excitedly, some with apprehension and concern, the whole thing looking like a covert operation they had seen in a movie.

But Julian watched with empathy as one hysterical lady cried into the chest of a consoling police officer. One of the victims was probably her child.

The ME, a tall, heavyset man, in his thirties, approached the student sprawled over the doorframe. He performed a quick check of the man's pulse with a finger at the throat, next to the gaping wound. He shook his head. The man was dead.

With brisk, quiet steps, except for crunching glass, he moved through the door, and walked to the prone body of the killer. He made no indication of surveying the restaurant in any obvious attempt to glimpse Julian. He performed the same test, quickly feeling for a pulse. His expression again indicated – dead. He did the same for the rest of the bodies. When he reached the children, he shook his head. Julian, behind the trashcan, watched the ME's lips grimace as he checked each child for a pulse. All were dead.

He went to the unconscious girl. Carefully probing her stomach. She grimaced with a moan, but did not regain consciousness. He motioned toward the door and the waiting medics, and motioned them to come through the door to pick up the girl.

The medics, in their white uniforms, rushed toward the door, carrying the fold-up stretchers. Again, glass crunched underfoot as they hurried to their tasks of checking and retrieving bodies.

Julian stood back, watching from around the corner, the same spot from which he had witnessed only moments earlier the horror that had turned his life upside down.

Very quickly, the first pair carefully lifted the girl, placed her on the gurney, and strapped her to it. The somber medics headed for the missing door amid glass and pools of blood. Then, outside, past hopeful parents, miscellaneous onlookers, and working their way through the crowd of policemen and vehicles, finally reaching the ambulance.

In a matter of seconds, the wailing of desperate sirens broke the silence that had taken over the area except for the occasional communications on the police speakers.

The medics were professionals. Removing the bodies, they did not attempt to look toward the back, get a glimpse of the possible maniac. They did what they were trained for. Retrieved the victims from their treacherous surroundings. Not that it mattered anymore for these victims.

One by one, stretcher-by-stretcher, the bloody victims were removed from the once busy restaurant now turned into a mausoleum full of bodies.

Because the bearded man Julian had shot was the oldest of the victims, his body was removed last.

The impulse was growing stronger. He wanted to know the name of the man he had shot and killed. Should I do it? Should I just rush over to the body and give the wallet a quick yank and be done with it? But he had waited too long.

The medics now approached the body, and Julian moved forward cautiously and pointed, saying, "That's the man who did all this...who killed all these people." He wanted to ask them to pull the wallet and just simply tell him the identification of the man lying there. But the thought of any move by him at this point seemed monumental, very aggressive.

"I would appreciate it if you would mention that to the man in charge outside." Not knowing exactly how to respond, the two medics stood motionless for a brief moment, then nodded at Julian that they understood his request. They placed the stretcher on the floor and, placing the bloodied corpse into a body bag, zipped the bag, and carefully placed it on the stretcher.

They started to move out the door when Julian said, "I admit that I shot that man, the one you're holding...." He paused for a second considering his words, realizing his statement would be hard to swallow by anyone they told. "I did this...using his own gun that I knocked from his hands. But it was in self-defense. After he had shot all the other people. *He was going to shoot me*," he said, sudden urgency in his voice. "That's all." The medics nodded again and quickly walked through the front door, toward the waiting crowd.


*9:50AM McDonald's*

Numbness was setting in, especially in Julian's mind. He thought about his cerebral synapses struggling with reality. He realized he was being incredibly analytical about his thoughts.

Everything appeared to be in slow motion. It seemed like hours had passed. But only thirty minutes had lapsed since the first shot was fired. It was probably shock, he figured. Like watching a wreck as it happened. Time suddenly stands still.

He looked around the restaurant at the leftover carnage, blood was everywhere. He had just lost his parents - today he felt he was losing his mind. The attic would be a nice place to be right about now.

And they were no help at all. Not one whisper. Why won't you distract me like you've been doing all these years? He smiled again, but the smile almost erupted into tears of despair. He inhaled a deep breath. Shit. He exhaled a long sigh. What a fucked up day, he thought bitterly.

"Unit 7, this is HQ." The noise snapped Julian out of his fog.

"This is Lieutenant Brown. Go ahead, HQ."

"We have the information requested, it collaborates with the facts Mr. Barrin gave. We're working on a more thorough background, family history, that sort of thing."

"Let me know what else you find. We know where he lives, is this correct?"

"10-4, Lieutenant. GC is headed that way."

"Good. Maybe now we'll get some real answers. Unit 7 over and out."

"HQ out."

A black van containing a special police force pulled up in front of a large old house at 2322 Manchester. This was known as the Ground Cover Unit. Three men emerged from the van and for five seconds their eyes panned the house looking for signs of life and the best points of entry. Then they went into action, moving swiftly, decisively, in different directions surrounding Julian's house.

"Julian. This is Lieutenant Brown. So far your information checks out. They'll run a check on the man you claim is the killer. We're also running a more thorough check on you. If everything jives, you'll only be taken downtown for normal questioning, and released. Fair enough?"

"Sounds good, Lieutenant. I hope you're right." The thought of a thorough check would have put Julian at ease if not for the nagging thought, that hopefully they would not find out about 1890 and Julian Barrin.

# CHAPTER 6

*10:20AM McDonald's*

Just when Julian thought things couldn't get any worse, a van pulled in behind the squad cars. The first thing he noticed was the logo on its side. KARK TV4. Within minutes a parabolic dish was raised on its top, and a crew of three men pulled a camera, cables, and other news paraphernalia from inside the van.

Julian recognized the reporter, Bob Day, as one he had watched on the news at 10. Another man hoisted a camera, including backpack, to his shoulders, snapped it in place, and lifted a cover from the goggle-eyed lens. The man tested the zooming mechanism, and, satisfied with the action, turned to Bob.

Julian watched as the cameraman spoke into a small collar mike, then he reached up and flipped a switch on the back of the portable recorder. The unit was now beaming a live report via the dish and satellite linkup. Fifteen miles away, the control room at KARK was full of operators who quickly adjusted the color spectrum.

With the camera rolling, and the cameraman pacing the

newsman, they approached Lieutenant Brown with big smiles. They shook hands and the reporter clapped Brown on the shoulder. Obviously these scenes were old hat for the two men.

Enthralled, Julian watched Brown nod, and eyebrows raise, as he appeared to utter a warning to the newsman that Julian couldn't make out.

Newsman Bob Day had an earplug stuffed in his left ear, listening to cues from Control. "Remember Bob, we'll have tapes rolling at 10:55 so you can continue, and we'll break away for Washington." Bob stiffened proudly, and smiled. It was a busy day in Little Rock.

The reporter pointed to his cameraman and lifted the microphone to his lips, quickly adjusting his confident smile to a somber face. Quite tall, the young cameraman crouched and became the reporter's shadow as they walked beside the playground fronting McDonald's.

Several policemen pulled guns from their shiny black holsters, preparing to cover the reporter in the event the supposed maniac inside the restaurant decided to add to the body count.

Julian's knees nearly buckled; he had witnessed the first real sign of how bad things were for him at that moment. He was headline news, guns were aimed his way, and everyone was probably betting he wouldn't leave McDonald's alive.

Taking a deep, ragged breath, Julian's eyes began to alternate between the spectacle outside just a few feet away and the television set on the counter behind him where the face of Bob Day was surreal.

Standing just twenty feet away, the reporter, staring at the camera, began his report. Julian was certain Bob's eyes were alternating ever so slightly between the camera and his news subject

"This should be a day of festivity and celebration for our great nation and especially for the proud natives of Arkansas and this capital city. However, just minutes ago, a tragedy occurred across the street from the University of Arkansas and only a few feet from where I stand.

"As the world watches the inauguration of Arkansas' own governor Bill Clinton being sworn in as our great nation's 52nd president of the United States, a tragedy right here threatens to overshadow this momentous event.

"We will, of course, break away from this report to join the ceremony. I will continue coverage of this tragedy, and the report will be aired later."

Julian could hear every word from the reporter's location and on the television behind him. Everything was larger than life, surreal, and he was in the center of it, the impact suddenly fierce inside his heart with the knowledge that he had stopped the presses, so to speak. He knew everyone's eyes were glued to their television or their ears to the radio, waiting for something incredible to happen before their eyes and ears.

The report opened with Bob Day staring into the camera, the golden arches of the McDonald's restaurant looming behind him. Julian couldn't help watching both events, the one outside and the one on the counter television. They should be the same, but they seemed different.

"Bob Day reporting live from McDonald's restaurant on University Avenue just across the street from the university campus. Every story has a beginning, a middle, and an end. The story that's about to unfold here is one with a bizarre twist, a very strange and violent beginning, and a very sad middle that is unfolding as we speak.

"According to police officials, pools of blood are everywhere. Also, according to police, the alleged killer is waiting inside, refusing to come out. We may witness the ending this very hour."

Jesus, thought Julian. Killer. He makes it sound so hopeless.

"You always think that catastrophes such as this one that occurred in our front yard, happen to other people, other countries. However, at approximately 8:40 a.m. this morning, 21 young people, including five children aged ten, were murdered in cold blood by a...what? A maniac! A wild man! A terrorist! A killer! And on police reports the man will be called what he is and was this morning, a gunman who will go down in history as the first to commit this atrocity, in the first mass slaying that America has experienced.

Julian was hyperventilating and broke out in a cold sweat. All eyes of the world were on him. He heard Bob Day's every derogatory word in slow motion and he thought he would faint. This reporter was painting him as exactly what he figured he was thanks to ancestors haunting his attic, and Professor Dawson and his exciting psychology class. A madman! His ancestors left him a lineage he couldn't deny this morning because the world was his witness and they figured without a doubt he is a madman. A killer! Shit!

"The alleged gunman did allow medics to retrieve the only survivor and the bodies of those who died. Names are being withheld until next of kin are notified. Lieutenant Brown, of the Little Rock police department, has informed me that the alleged gunman's name is Julian Barrin who lives in Little Rock. I can actually see the alleged gunman staring through the wrecked door, staring at this reporter.

At this point the camera panned to the door and Julian, zooming in on his face. Horrified and embarrassed, Julian almost panicked. He glanced at the counter and saw his own profile, and something he wished he did not see - the gun tucked in his belt, for the entire world to see! He turned slightly so the gun disappeared from view. But was he too late, had everyone already seen the weapon?

Bob Day continued.

"The bizarre twist in this incredible story is an unbelievable account by the suspect himself. Julian apparently denies the act of mass murder, and indeed, declares that he is in fact a hero, that he interrupted the gunman and shot him, apparently fatally, using the gunman's own weapon, indeed, possibly the gun you may have seen moments ago tucked inside his belt.

Julian froze and his heart pounded. That would not help his situation. He glanced at the parking lot expecting to see guns drawn and pointed at his head, but all was seemingly quiet, no one seemed to be responding or reacting to Bob's report. He looked at the counter and again saw his own profile; the camera was pointed at him again. Even though the weather was cool, the audience could see nervous perspiration had formed on the hero's or perhaps the villain's face. Those at home were possibly voting. Hero. Villain.

Julian looked past the entourage surrounding the restaurant that had become a sepulcher of mass death moments earlier and across the street at the tall buildings of the campus. "Jesus. I wonder what Professor Dawson is thinking about all of this," Julian suddenly pondered. The thought caused disappointment to shower into his mind.

This has not been a good morning. Disappointment over the intrusion of his sanctity, and now this. He was very fond of the professor, considered him a mentor as he was Julian's advisor. He knew the professor had great expectations of him.

Dawson was aware of his student's obsession with the human mind. He wasn't completely aware of the reasons. Or, maybe he is, thought Julian, maybe he's smarter than I give him credit for.

At that very moment, across University Avenue, deep inside the university campus, the dean of the psychology department, Professor Philip Dawson, was prompted by his secretary to turn on his television. "The reporter said it was Julian Barrin, Doctor Dawson."

*I'm not surprised this has happened. I was warned, kind of,* thought Dawson. *But how do you tell anyone something like this - as a prophecy, for Christ's sake.* "It's a mistake," the professor muttered to himself, flicking the remote to turn on the television on his credenza. Dawson flicked the remote to Channel 4, stared in disbelief for a pregnant moment, and under his breath, cried, *"Oh God."* *It's worse than I imagined.*

Barrin's blue eyes stared back at Professor Dawson. The camera zoomed in closer and the concern and fear were obvious in Julian's face. Wide eyed, Dawson bit his lower lip, not believing what was unfolding just across the street from his office, not to mention what he was witnessing in his favorite student.

"This is unbelievable," said Dawson, frowning at the television and shaking his head in disbelief. *I really didn't think it would be this bad. Damn those psychotic, neurotic people. Well, Julian, these are the guys you want to be intimate with. So be it.*

*Hell, listen to me...I teach this shit!*

Ruth left her desk and approached Dawson's office tentatively. She saw the professor leaning over his desk, watching the breaking news, contemplating. "I'm so sorry. Do you think-"

"Hell no," said Dawson, eyes glued to the action. "You've known him as long as anyone else here."

"Have you heard the details though?" said Ruth. "Pretty incriminating evidence. It's like...he's the only one left alive, except for that girl, and she's in bad shape..."

"He didn't do it." *Of course you knew it would get this bad. You were warned.*

The professor reached for the telephone.

# CHAPTER 7

Each GC man covered one of the three levels of the old house, carefully, painstakingly, checking every drawer, every closet, every nook and cranny. They knocked on the walls, knowing from their training and experience that these old houses sometimes had secret holdings in the walls, or even secret passageways to the basement and to the outside world.

They were working in sync, exploring anything that looked like it might hold a clue when the report came through their wireless headsets. "HQ here. We've received some rather interesting information. Be extra careful when you approach the attic...repeat, be extra careful when you approach the attic.

"A professor Dawson, Dean of psychology at UALR just called and told the chief a pretty far out story. Seems a locker in the attic contains some interesting material and maybe...more. He wouldn't elaborate, but he said it was pretty far out and that we would probably understand...eventually.

"He also said he had a...feeling that this would happen -

the McDonald's thing. HQ out."

"That's all? No further elaboration? Not going to bring him in for questioning?" said the leader.

"You know what we know. Chief says we don't touch the professor."

"Sounds like spooky-shit to me," said the leader.

The GC unit continued their search.

The attic would be covered last.

# CHAPTER 8

*10:43AM Baptist Memorial Hospital*

Eight miles away at Baptist Hospital off the 430 Freeway, the young girl who seemed to be Julian's only hope and whom all of Little Rock was concerned about was being wheeled from the operating room and into intensive care. A reporter was on the scene, following the girl with a cameraman who kept the sedated girl in view for all to see, including Julian.

"The young girl who was the only fortunate victim of the bizarre shooting at McDonald's and whose identity remains unknown was checked for internal hemorrhaging and it was discovered that the bullet went completely through her body and apparently didn't damage any vital organs. She lost a lot of blood and will remain in intensive care for further observation.

"She apparently carried no identification, so identification will be attempted through dental records if necessary...."

"Thank God," Julian breathed a sigh of relief. "Maybe now she'll be okay and can tell them the truth."

The report continued with the usual repeats and speculations.

*10:45AM McDonald's*


At McDonald's via continued satellite link and the Channel 4 news van parked just yards away, Bob Day was cued by police headquarters to follow up with an update.

The cameraman, moving like Bob's shadow, was ready. The red light flicked on, indicating on the air.

"Police apparently are gathering information at this time to confirm or refute Julian Barrin's denial of his part in this terrible tragedy."

The reporter nodded and pointed with his free hand, the cue for the cameraman to zoom in and pan the front of McDonald's. Viewers were given their first glimpse at the results of the violence. "You can see broken glass everywhere. Moments earlier medics recovered the body of a victim who was shot in the neck and was found sprawled across this doorframe. The man's identity is being withheld, but it is known that he was a student at the university majoring in science. Fifteen other bodies also were taken away to the morgue for a total of 21 victims of this morning's unbelievable tragedy."


*10:50AM McDonald's*


"This report was supposed to be taped while Channel 4 ran the preparation for the inauguration; however, circumstance dictate staying live."

The reporter held his position thirty feet away from the front of the restaurant. "The Governor of Arkansas is about to realize a dream, and become a hero for all of Arkansas. This reporter has learned that during heated and emotional debates, it was stated by many that maybe Julian is the hero or possibly that we are just willing victims. Inside McDonald's, the man of this tragic hour, Julian Barrin, claims he is innocent, indeed, that he disarmed the real gunman and is a hero, but one thing is certain, the bodies removed were definitely not willing victims-"

"Will you talk with me?" asked Julian, suddenly appearing in the doorway, his own nervous, alien voice, startling him. He quickly stepped back from the door when he noticed all guns being pulled and aimed, while the officers shielded themselves behind their cars.

The cameraman was good. He turned to catch the re-porter's emotions and reaction to Julian's request.

The reporter's eyes were wide with fear and excitement, his mouth in a tight smile, considering his next action. This was the chance newsmen waited for all their lives. To be able to inter-view a potential killer on the scene. "People, the voice you may have just heard, was the voice of the alleged suspect."

He took three cautious steps forward, turning his head, looking with uncertainty back at Brown, the cameraman piv-oting to shoot whatever the reporter looked at. Brown waved the reporter back, shaking his head adamantly.

"Get the hell out of there!" yelled Lieutenant Brown. Adrenaline rushed as firearms went off safety. Several closest to the front gripped their pistols, pulled back arming mecha-nisms, loading shells into their chambers. Five 38 Special-caliber police guns now had a shell in the chamber, safeties off. All over Little Rock, housewives, mechanics, lawyers, doc-tors, and students were glued to their sets, watching for any action.

The reporter waved back at Brown, and tentatively stepped three more paces forward. Brown, not anxious to step into the line of fire, afraid of possibly exciting or upsetting the suspect, held his position and watched carefully.

The cameraman angled his camera to focus on the front of the restaurant, through the shattered door facing, creating a portal in which to view the horrible spectacle. Viewers at home gasped as they saw, in color, a face move into camera range. The killer? Opinions varied, but certain of his guilt were families and friends of those who lost their lives inside the res-taurant that morning.

The camera zoomed in. Now the viewers were getting what they hoped for. Wide blue eyes clearly visible, blond hair that had been brushed that morning, tussled now from nerv-ous rubbing the past forty-five minutes. Definitely a maniac many opined; a scared victim opted others.

# CHAPTER 9

*10:52AM Barrin Residence*

**A**GC man stood at the top of the stairs looking up at an attic door. Beside him a brown rope snaked down a wall to a retainer. The man called to the other two men for backup. When they appeared at the bottom of the stairs, he motioned to the rope and gave a pulling sign, and pointed up. The men nodded and with catlike movements were at the man's side in the blink of an eye.

Meanwhile, the world watched the presidential inauguration, and Little Rock, Arkansas, residents watched the continuation of horror in their own 'backyard' live on their television sets.

*11:07AM McDonald's*

Bob motioned with an index finger to a well-trained crew. It was their signal to break away for exactly one minute. The camera kept rolling while Control broke for a promo of the inauguration.

"You're clear, Bob," the voice of a Control operator stated in his earphone.

Bob stared through the empty doorframe at Julian who had stuck the gun behind him in his pants, not wanting the viewers to see the weapon and possibly strengthen their opinion that he was indeed the killer. He sat with one hand under the table, the other resting on top of the table. The posture insinuating to only the reporter that he may have a weapon out of sight. "Mr. Barrin, please, may we sit and talk like civilized people?"

Julian forced a smile and motioned toward a yellow table for two, the table being on the other side of the room from where the deceased gunman had started his wild rampage killing almost everyone. The cameraman remained outside, the lens poking through the doorframe, like a mechanical canine sniffing for danger ahead. He couldn't see the cameraman's face, but Julian knew the camera was focusing on him, video and audio rolling, intent to capture the moment and every nuance about his surreal news subject.

The reporter quickly considered the situation. Brown's squad car was too far away from the van to have the lieutenant ambling over for a conversation. Bob spoke into his microphone. "Patch me to Lieutenant Brown's car, immediately!" The console operator in the van threw a switch that put the reporter on a phone patch. He dialed a number at the police station, connecting him to a dispatcher he had called on many occasions but none so violent as today.

"Police dispatch. This is officer Robinson. How can I help you?"

"Betty - Frank, with KARK."

"Frank. What are you up to-"

"We're covering the McDonald's murder scene *live*," he interrupted. He urgently filled her in. "Bob is talking with the suspect as we speak. He needs to talk to the lieutenant immediately!" he stated with the same priority his newsman had.

She exhausted a heavy sigh. "It never stops, does it?"

"Betty, we don't have a moment to waste!" he urged the dispatcher. A second later he heard a ringing. His reporter was being patched through.

# CHAPTER 10

*11:09AM.*

The control operator at KARK was watching the end of the promo approach, listening simultaneously to the conversation. He had thirty seconds.

Outside the van, crouched next to his squad car, Lieutenant Brown was stewing, wondering what the hell was happening when his phone rang. "Who the hell-"

"It's me in the van, Lieutenant. I'm patching you through to Bob." One click later the newsman and the lieutenant were linked.

"Are you crazy, Bob?"

*15 seconds.*

"Hold on, Lieutenant. I just wanted to let you know the situation. I'm okay," he looked ruefully at Julian, the camera still rolling. "Julian Barrin and I are talking. He's very calm. I'm having my cameraman stand outside the door using his zoom, so if anything should happen, he'll be able-"

"I get the picture."

*On the air.* The lieutenant and the reporter were linked and being transmitted.

"Good luck, you crazy bastard." Eyebrows went up on the people at Control. Hearing Brown's expletive, the viewers gasped and quickly turned up their sets. Never had anyone witnessed such a spectacle.

The newsman sat for a moment, scrutinizing his situation, not afraid for his own safety, but curious about the truth. Was this relatively calm man sitting before him really a hero? Or was he a violent killer moments earlier and was he sitting there with a gun in his hidden hand?

As if reading the reporter's mind, Julian decided to give up the defensive posture. He slowly, carefully, slid his right hand from under the table and, just as slowly, brought it to rest on top of the table.

"Hi, I'm Bob Day," the reporter introduced himself, smiling, and carefully offering his hand. Julian smiled tentatively and reached out while moving with care to shake Bob's hand.

The two men stared at each other momentarily, the camera catching every action, every word, and neither was aware that at that very moment three men from the GC unit were covering every inch of Julian's house, looking for answers, for anything that would shed new light on the sketchy information they had. "We're live," the reporter smiled apologetically, "well, we're being recorded, but we're broadcasting locally while the rest of the world is watching the inauguration, so everything you...we say, will be documented and aired nationwide after the inauguration."

Julian nodded, his upper teeth playing with his lower lip in contemplation.

"Is there anything you'd like to say?" said the reporter, glancing at his cameraman for an instant, a habit to make sure all attention was on his interview, the camera was still rolling, and the mike was still hot. The red light on the front of the camera said yes to all his concerns.

"Just that..." Julian turned to face the camera, "just that I did not shoot all these people...these, these *children*," said Julian incredulously. He looked around the restaurant as though searching for a clue, an answer to his plight. Back at the camera.

"I was almost shot by the gunman. I used a food tray to slap the gun away from him. Then I ran and grabbed the gun off the floor." Julian was looking now at the spot across the room by the door where all the heart pounding action had taken place. And remembering the moment; now it was being documented.

His stomach churned with gut wrenching adrenaline that poured in making his heart race. His breath got away from him for a moment. He took a deep breath. Everyone at home was watching glued to their sets and engrossed by the saga happening just miles from their safe havens, trying to imagine what it must be like, the horror, the fear. All form of citizens including the police and survivors of victims.

Attitudes of viewers ran the gamut, from one end of the spectrum to the other. Sympathy and teeth-grinding anger.

Stop him. Help him. Kill him.

"I'm a student at the university - not a killer," said Julian adamantly, his eyes now showing fatigue that everyone could see. Some shook their heads in sympathy, others, convinced that he was probably guilty, just watched in contempt.

"Bob, this is Brown."

The reporter's face didn't budge, didn't show any sign of the page he heard from the monitor plugged into his left ear.

"Bob, this is Lieutenant *Brown*." Bob ignored the call and the growing impatience in the voice and continued his vigil, knowing Brown's impatience would soon turn to raw anger.

The unit was still transmitting, the camera still recording, and Julian was finishing his speech. "....I just want to set the record straight before I leave this restaurant. I don't want everyone to think I'm guilty and end up in jail where I can't help myself. This is my only hope as I see it. I am not the killer."

Bob Day glanced at his cameraman and lifted his eyebrows. The camera moved only slightly to bring Bob into view with Julian still somewhat visible. "Julian, are you saying that you intend to hold your stand here until you come up with proof that you are innocent?"

There was a moment of silence while Julian considered his words carefully though he had already stated his intentions earlier on tape. Bob's question simply put extra emphasis on his precarious situation. "I don't think I can do it any other way, Bob. I have to wait as long as I can and hope something develops. Maybe the girl will be able to tell them the truth."

"Thanks for being candid, Julian. We'll take a break and let the audience at home join the inauguration for a moment. This is Bob Day with Julian Barrin, a man claiming innocence and that he is actually a hero, but suspected by police as being the person who shot and killed 21 people while one other person survived besides Julian. We'll continue reporting live in a moment."

The control room was able to break fairly clean, joining the inauguration at a timely spot.

"Julian, I'm going to call Brown and ask him if there's any word on the girl," said Bob, hoping an explanation would defuse any possible anxiety his news subject might be capable of experiencing. Though he held strong doubts of Julian's guilt, he knew nothing of Julian's propensity for violence. He realized that this man was a desperate man who at the moment was acting civilized, but in perhaps an hour when patience and time ran out for the people outside, he might be like a caged cheetah, ready to strike with uncontrollable rage. A scenario he didn't want to chance.

Julian thought for a moment, glanced at the still rolling camera, and with a look of renewed hope in his eyes, nodded. "Okay. That sounds good. Excuse me, Bob." He stood up and walked to the counter where he poured a cup of water from a drinking fountain. Bob noticed the gun in Julian's belt and figured that was what the trip to the counter was about. Playing his cards...carefully.

Bob also knew that he wasn't going to report it to Brown-- for some reason he didn't feel he needed to.

# CHAPTER 11

*11:13AM The Locker In the Attic*

The three GC men had explored the attic and now stood near the small window, preparing to open the locker. The eerie report from HQ and experience told them it had recently been opened. It made searching the locker even more appealing. They also knew there could be a bomb inside and this could be the grand finale of a madman - to blow up the local police elite after having killed off numerous citizens.

All were trained in bomb disposal procedures.

They nodded at each other and actually flipped a coin to decide who would search while the others watched.

The winner bent down and began the ritual of searching under the presumption that there was a bomb inside.

The specialist ran his hands carefully through the air on all sides of the locker in search of very thin and barely visible trip wires. He scrutinized every external crevice of the locker before ever touching the lock. He then tackled the underneath portion with equal care. Once the locker was clear for exploring, he would perform intensive fingerprinting.

*11:15AM McDonald's*

Julian couldn't wait any longer. He walked to a pay phone in the corner and dialed the campus, asking for the psychology department. Ten seconds later, he had Dawson on the phone.

"Julian, are you okay?"

"I'm as good as I can be under the circumstances, Dr. Dawson. I just wanted you to know that I did not do this."

"I knew that. I know a lot more than even you, perhaps."

Julian was perplexed. "What in the world are you talking about, Dr. Dawson?"

"Your parents called me a few months ago. They enlightened me about several things. They explained that you held high regard for me and wanted to let me know that you might need a friend who would understand someday. Well, looks like that day has come, Julian."

With his cameraman taping all of his moves, the reporter went to the back of the restaurant near the restroom, walking carefully around pools of blood that were drying but still left horrible stains. He sat at a booth to make a private call to Brown on his wireless unit.

Within a minute, he was having a recorded conversation with the lieutenant, explaining that things were under control and Julian was level headed so far. He asked about the girl and was told that a police reporter was at the hospital gathering details.

The lieutenant's voice went lower, softer. "Uh, Bob."

"What are you thinking, Lieutenant?"

"You're right, Bob. I have something on my mind." The patrol leader inhaled a deep breath. "Okay, Bob, tell me this. Do you think, I mean think, there's any way...that-"

"Can you take him? Is that what you want to know? Is he too dangerous, do I think he's guilty, etc." The reporter glanced at his cameraman and winked. The man's face was hidden behind his portable unit, but Bob knew he was smiling at the situation."

"Brown, I...I uh, can't say for sure, but I think he's probably innocent - as crazy as this whole thing seems. But I'm going solely on intuition. There is a lot of blood in here and he's still, uh, excited, and maybe excitable." He took a deep breath, realizing he had almost said his news subject was carrying a gun, but to say it in that way would have been irresponsible reporting. He felt a closeness to Julian that he couldn't explain.

"Could you take him? I don't know. I don't know if he's capable of responding, or if it would bluff him and he would lay down arms." The reporter was shaking his head, "I just don't know. He seems very determined."

"Bob, are you milking this thing?" said Brown.

"I know you're kidding when you say that."

# CHAPTER 12

*11:19AM Locker in the Attic*

The GC unit finished checking the locker and had a collection of fingerprints to send in for analysis. They had a remote unit that would transmit the prints so they would have results in minutes if the fingerprints were on file at Quantico.

That wasn't all. They had read relevant portions of the journal that lent to an attitude of genetic pre-dispositioned mental disorders. This concerned them, no matter what they had heard from HQ. As far as they were concerned, any fingerprints that brought back bad news, their owner should be checked out immediately. They also were sending pages that would lend to a quick personality profile. Quantico's behavioral lab specialty. The leader pressed the button and the unit began transmitting. First the documents for the FBI's files, then the fingerprints.

The light was blinking red for about two minutes, suddenly clicking to solid green. A match from the files of the FBI. This meant someone had a felony record and had been inside the locker. Now they would have a name to report.

*11:32AM McDonald's*

Lieutenant Brown called Bob to express his concern about the reporter's safety.

"Bob, Julian is probably what he says he is, but, I can't risk assuming that with you in there. If things turn for the worse, you could end up a hostage and that would make my job a lot more difficult. I need you out of there so-" Brown was interrupted, to Bob's chagrin.

"What's going on?" Hearing no response, Bob called out again "Brown-"

"Bob. Put me on." Bob was surprised but elated. The lieutenant was there and ready for an update.

*11:48AM McDonald's*

"The hospital called and the girl is groggy, but awake. They now know she is a deaf mute, Bob."

"You don't say?" Bob waved frantically at his cameraman and gestured for a live mike, which meant send both sides of his conversation to the air - now!

The cameraman didn't miss a beat. Flipping a switch he focused on Bob while angling his position for his reporter to be on screen along with the man of the hour - Julian. The cameraman nodded.

The control room people were frantically getting permission to leave the inauguration for the live update.

# CHAPTER 13

*12:02PM Control Room*

**P**ermission granted.

"You've got 15 seconds Remote. And we do have a short take from the hospital that you need to cue us for. It's exactly 30 seconds long." The inauguration was now being recorded for later transmission while the McDonald's standoff was about to take live to the air.

The cameraman rapidly held up five fingers three times, then began the digit countdown.

"...five, four, three, two, one" the cameraman quietly cued, along with the left index finger finally pointing at the re-porter.

"This is Bob Day with an unexpected update from McDonald's on University Avenue across from the Little Rock campus.

Julian watched the counter TV, alternately shifting his eyes between the actual report just 10 feet away and the transmitted report on the counter TV. He noted that the camera had him in its peripheral and he was in the background for all the viewing audience to see. He didn't budge.

"We have an interesting fact to reveal to our listeners, one that won't be such great news to our news subject, Julian Barrin." Bob glanced at Julian who was standing by the counter, watching and listening intently.

"This reporter has just learned from the hospital that the only survivor - indeed, the only live witness - of this morning's tragedy, a young girl, whose name hasn't been determined yet, is out of intensive care and appears to be off the critical list. However, there is an interesting development in this bizarre incident. One that will undoubtedly delay resolution to young Julian's situation."

No one dared flinch and breaths were held all over Little Rock as everyone waited for this crucial update. "We are told that the girl...is a deaf mute. Let's go to Memorial Hospital now for an on the spot update."

Julian's mouth dropped open and he almost forgot he was on screen, his knees nearly buckling out from under him.

At this moment, right on cue, a prerecorded tape of the girl being whisked to a recovery room was played, showing the girl's form under the sheet on the moving gurney.

*15 seconds.* Nurses and doctors were seen quickly shuffling out of camera range, concern and indignation reflecting from their faces.

*Five seconds.* The camera zoomed to the shooting victim's face revealing that she was asleep and under heavy sedation.

"The scene you just saw was recorded only ten minutes earlier. Police have stationed a communications specialist named Karen Childress from the school for the deaf with her. She's sitting in the IC room next to the bed, waiting for the girl to become conscious; otherwise authorities won't be able to trust anything she says. I'll keep you posted. Bob Day reporting."

### The attic at the Barrin residence

The man's picture was transmitted along with all vitals from Quantico. After what had transpired at McDonald's that morning, the name connected to fingerprints and the photo was the most interesting part, and the information provided with the name raised all eyebrows. They also had read some of the journal Julian used so religiously in his yearly rituals. It was history, the subjects all deceased by now, but the bizarre information detailed within was relevant. The GC leader called in their findings to Little Rock police HQ.

After listening to the details, the chief ordered the GC unit to call the restaurant immediately to advise Lieutenant Brown of his decision concerning the standoff and the alleged killer. The evidence was in Julian's favor. They would hold off on any aggressive action and wait for word from the hospital.

# CHAPTER 14

*12:38PM*

The fax machine in the Baptist Memorial Hospital rang and began buzzing. A fax was about to come through. As the document oozed slowly out of the device, the desk nurse read the cover page. The fax was addressed to Karen Childress.

*12:50PM McDonald's*

With all eyes including those of police and bystanders focusing on the opening where a glass door was shattered by bullets and a falling body, no one paid attention to the squat figure approaching from the south, the least protected side of the restaurant.

The figure was wearing tattered clothing including an old fatigue jacket with lots of deep pockets, and a hat with the brim pulled over his forehead. Whoever it was, approached in a very casual manner until he or she was within twenty yards of the nearest police car. At this point the hat fell off when suddenly the left hand reached inside the left pocket and pulled out an object with a piece of cloth attached. The right hand had a lighter that was already burning. The flame was quickly touched to the cloth, which immediately burned indicating that it was soaked with gasoline - the content of the bottle the cloth snaked from. It was a Molotov cocktail!

The figure suddenly ran as close as possible screaming "You son of a bitch," tossing the flaming missile toward the entrance. The bottle was lofted higher than the restaurant but with an angle that put it as close to the front door as possible under the circumstances, indicating the person had previous experience with this sort of thing. Every officer reacted by reflex. Guns were pulled that weren't already out, and desperate shots were fired at the bottle in mid air. The first half dozen shots either missed or nicked the potential bomb. One shot made contact and the bottle exploded with a mild whoosh, and flames covered the sidewalk, barely missing the front entrance.

The figure that had tossed the now defunct bomb was lying face down on the pavement, not moving, apparently to avoid any spray of glass or stray bullets. When an officer approached with handcuffs in one hand, a 45 in the other, he placed a knee in the back of the suspect to prevent any further action or possible resistance; the abrupt pressure caused a moan of pain. In a firm voice, he commanded the prone figure to put his hands behind his head. The figure obliged. That was when the officer saw the nails of the hands were painted red. It was a woman.

# CHAPTER 15

*1 PM Baptist Hospital*

**K**aren Childress pressed the call button.
A policeman opened the door and let the nurse enter. The nurse motioned for the officer to join them. The reporter was asked to remain outside.

The girl who had been shot just a few hours before was awake.

The three of them gathered close to the girl's bed.

The shooting victim was still somewhat groggy but becoming more alert and didn't appear to be frightened anymore. She smiled at the nurse and the specialist, some trepidation in her face.

"Do you know where you are?" said the nurse, who deferred to the specialist.

*What is your name?* Karen signed to the girl, who immediately showed relief for having someone to relate to. Everyone watched intently to discover the name of the mystery girl who had been shot just hours before at McDonald's across from the university campus.

She signed rapidly at first, and then she slowed down and

repeated herself.

*Barbara...*

*Jean...*

*Haden.*

Karen stepped closer and shook the girl's hand.

"Nice to meet you finally, Barbara Jean Haden," said Karen, smiling broadly. An officer in the corner used his two-way radio to call the station, reporting what he had just learned. He then opened the door and motioned to the reporter who hurried through the door with his cameraman.

News was on the run again in the hospital and Barbara was again the center of attention. The room was awash in the spotlight and at first Barbara shielded her face, then the cameraman angled his light swivel slightly to avoid blinding his subject but still with enough light for a clear transmission.

"We're going live for just a moment, if that's okay with everyone," said the reporter. "Just long enough to have her say her name on the air and give us a quick account of how she feels." He pointed to the nurse. "You could give a very quick medical report if you like." The nurse nodded, smiling, casually checking her hair in the mirror behind Karen.

"Thirty seconds, people and we'll be on for one minute."

Karen signed that the nurse would check her vitals and the officer would be a witness to their conversation. The girl nodded.

The girl then signed to Karen that she didn't remember very much about the incident at McDonald's except seeing a lot of children being shot and then feeling pain and passing out.

*You probably went into shock,* signed Karen.

The girl nodded.

*Do you know who shot you?*

The girl shook her head.

*I mean, would you know his face, I assume you don't know a name.*

Karen flicked on the television. Immediately, the coverage was on screen. The girl's eyes went wide. Julian was in the background as Bob Day reported. The sound was muted.

"Are you okay?" said Karen, signing as she spoke, concerned the face of Julian on the news report might scare her or even traumatize her.

She signed, *Yes, I'm okay*, her breathing a little fast and heavy.

"Was that the man?" said Karen, pointing at the screen.

The girl thought for a moment, frowning, remembering, fear coming into her face. The memory was obviously vivid as she started crying. She took a proffered napkin from the nurse, blew her nose. Then she signed, nodding that she probably could recognize the man who shot her.

"But was that the man," said Karen, watching the officer who was poised with his two-way, ready to report.

*But was that the man?* She signed.

"Maybe we should turn off the television," said the officer. "If that was the man who shot her-" But the girl shook her head adamantly, gesturing to the contrary. She had lip read what he said.

Karen touched the girl's shoulder, reassuring her as much as possible. She could tell that the girl was in some pain from being shot and the resulting operation.

"Ten seconds, people," said the reporter in a calm voice, watching the television and glancing at his cameraman, who was flicking his fingers in a countdown.

"Three, two, one...this is Ted Newman reporting live from Baptist Hospital in Little Rock, Arkansas, with a breaking news report." The cameraman turned the camera just enough to include Barbara in the picture from her hospital bed. "The lady who just appeared on your screen is the sole survivor of this morning's terrible tragedy at McDonald's across from the university campus."

The reporter walked over to the bedside. "We have finally learned the identify of the young lady." The camera turned to show just the patient in the hospital bed. "Viewers I would like for you to meet Barbara Jean Haden," said the reporter, shaking hands with her.

"This is the only victim who survived this morning's shooting." He motioned for the nurse to move forward. "This is nurse Remington. Could you give the viewers a quick medical breakdown of Barbara's condition, Nurse?"

"Yes, I will be happy to. The bullet passed through her in the abdominal region without causing any damage to vital organs. She is somewhat sedated for the bullet wound and the operation procedure. The exploratory operation lasted only twenty minutes and she was quickly brought to this room for recovery."

"Thank you nurse Remington," said the reporter, smiling at the camera. He glanced now and then at the television set as though confirming he was indeed transmitting live. "The necessity for speed in this case hardly needs explaining. There is a man named Julian Barrin who refuses to leave McDonald's until he is cleared of possible murder charges. If you have been watching you have seen the latest developments and we'll see how things turn out now that we have an actual witness."

He motioned to Karen to talk to Barbara and the listeners.

The specialist moved forward.

"I have a picture of a man..." *I have a picture of a man. See if you recognize him.*

"We are about to hear for the first time since the shooting from the victim's own...uh, sign language, what really happened, or at least who did the actual shooting." The camera focused solely on Karen and Barbara.

From her purse, Karen pulled a fresh photograph she received from the police an hour before that had been faxed to the hospital. The picture had been taken at the morgue. The man in the picture was lying on a prep gurney. She handed it to Barbara.

"Barbara, is this the man who shot you?" *Barbara, is this the man who shot you?* Karen was signing as rapidly as she could knowing a man's life was at stake.

The viewing audience, the Channel 4 control room, the whole world stopped breathing to capture this incredible moment, waiting for the shooting victim named Barbara - a deaf mute - to confirm or deny the allegations by police that they were holding a killer at bay in McDonald's restaurant.

# CHAPTER 16

*1:15PM McDonald's*

Lieutenant Brown put the microphone to his mouth. "Julian Barrin we've learned from the girl whose name is Barbara and corroborating evidence and resources that you are not the killer. You are free to come out as a free citizen."

The leader then dialed his phone. "Bob. This is Brown. Did you hear-" He inhaled a deep breath. "Good. Is he willing to come out now?"

At that time, a weary figure approached the door that had almost been engulfed in flames just moments before. He laid the gun on the sidewalk and backed to the left, toward the entourage of cars and officers, hands in the air, just as he had seen in the movies.

The cameraman and Bob Day were close behind Julian. "An irony to this tragic story, folks, is that this very television," the cameraman focused for a moment on the counter television, "was monitored by Julian as he awaited his fate, and now displays the back of Julian Barrin as he walks to freedom, leaving a building that housed a nightmare that the whole world, and especially, the good citizens of Little Rock, Arkansas, witnessed in disbelief just hours earlier."

"Julian, you're free, put your hands down, son," said Brown.

Viewers could see the man approaching the officers, his hands slowly coming back to his side. The reporter continued with his wrap up of the day's events. "...I repeat, an incredible afternoon, indeed, an incredible day, good for two...horrible for twenty one poor souls.

Day rushed forward, ahead of Julian, followed by his cameraman. "And now we capture the final moment of Julian walking away from a nightmare into a world that will never be the same for this University of Arkansas student."

"At least this story has a partially happy ending. Little Rock, Arkansas, has a new hero, one that hours earlier almost everyone was ready to...kill for revenge. Emotions can cloud the truth, and today the emotions were concentrated deep inside this capitol city in every person, hearts touched by death. Thanks to a lone survivor named Barbara Jean Haden, the truth was revealed just in time it seems.

"A Molotov cocktail was tossed at the restaurant just moments earlier in a desperate attempt to end the life of the very man who had saved the life of the only survivor of this morning's terrible tragedy.

"Julian Barrin is indeed a hero on this inauguration day."

# Epilogue

Viewers watched the back of Julian as he approached a squad car and Lieutenant Brown.

Bob continued his report. "As you see, Lieutenant Brown is offering Julian a ride, which the hero appears to be accepting. Wait a minute. Julian is waving at someone across University Avenue just as he's stepping into the vehicle. An unidentified man, possible a professor, is waving from the campus grounds.

"As I said earlier, every story has a beginning, a middle, and an end. Twenty one bodies were removed from this location this morning, a standoff took place, and Julian Barrin finally emerged from a tragedy at McDonald's and walked free, indeed, a hero, and now the police are putting the final touches on the crime scene."

The camera panned from Bob's face to the McDonald's restaurant. As you can see, the yellow police tape is being wrapped around the restaurant, banning people from crossing police lines. This landmark is now wrapped up and will have a place in criminal history forever, definitely in the minds of Little Rock, Arkansas, citizens forever.

The camera focused on the entrance. "There you see the entrance and the blackened spot left by the Molotov cocktail that was tossed by an angry woman, Kate Riddenour, we have just learned, who lost her only son, Tommy Riddenour, a seven year old, in today's shooting tragedy.

"Twenty one young people lost their lives here today at the hands of a gunman who went berserk for no apparent reason. This was another of the famed 'postal' syndromes where someone who feels life has dealt him a bad hand, decided to take other's lives in his own hands.

"Only one person, Barbara Jean Haden, lived to tell her story using sign language to communicate to specialist Karen Childress at Baptist Memorial Hospital where she remains, as we speak, in recovery. The camera moved back to focus on a close up of the reporter.

"This is Bob Day reporting live from McDonald's in Little Rock, Arkansas, on President Clinton's inauguration day."

The men rode silently, Julian in the front seat of the police car, reflecting, as Lieutenant Brown drove, headed for Julian's now infamous home in the northern part of Little Rock.

Taking a left on Rodney Parham, Julian broke the silence. "Lieutenant. I had to shoot and kill a man today." He looked the patrol captain in the eye. Brown glanced at his passenger hero expectantly. "I don't know his name. I need to know his name." The captain nodded slightly.

"You do know who he was?" *We know....* Julian cocked his head. The voice was gone as quickly as it had come. Or had it come at all. This was not the time for games, thought Julian. He managed a glimpse at Brown, but saw nothing to indicate he had heard. There was nothing to hear, he admonished himself.

Unaware of what was going on next to him, Brown glanced sideways at Julian, considering his question. "We know who he was, Julian. We first have to notify next of kin before releasing his name."

Julian nodded, thinking.

A moment later, Brown glanced back at his passenger and this time held his gaze a little longer. Julian stared forward in quiet resolve, seeing nothing in particular, tears streaming down his face. The lieutenant felt empathy. He had witnessed the same scene many times, especially in the officers - his own men. After having shot a suspect. It was never easy, never would be - he hoped.

"So when do you think I'll probably find out," said Julian softly, sniffling, wiping the tears with his sleeve.

"Probably tomorrow morning, first thing."

Julian nodded absently. "Is there anything you can tell me about him? Where he's from...did he have a family..?"

Brown stared ahead, tapping the steering wheel with both index fingers, silent for a moment. He finally smiled, and still looking ahead, said, "Tomorrow. Tomorrow, Julian, you'll find out more than you probably want to know." Julian's gaze abruptly left the window and jerked around to gaze upon Brown, a curious questioning look, but knowing he wasn't going to receive any answers until...tomorrow. He nodded to himself in silent acquiescence. He suddenly felt tired, worn out from the events of the day. But questions were filling his head that he couldn't stop. Curiosity was taking over his emotions. He wanted to know about the people he was forced to endure a day from hell with. Dead or alive.

"By the way, your professor friend called and put in a good word for you." Brown paused, eyeing Julian for a moment.

"I called him from the restaurant. He told me some pretty strange things, too, Lieutenant. He turned out to be a very good friend when I needed one."

"Yes he did," Brown stated matter of fact. "His input caused us to back off a little in our assumption."

They rode a little further. Julian's mind was careening with thoughts and questions he needed answers to.

"The lady who threw the bomb. She was trying to kill me. Why? Was one of those kids hers?"

"Kate Riddenour. She was a retired Marine," said Lieutenant Brown, sounding like he was talking to his squad, a monotone voice. "Had her son, seven year old Tommy while in the Marines. He was illegitimate by a colonel, but she was crazy about him." He paused, inhaled, and stared straight ahead, his lips pursed. "Looks like she just about went crazy after losing him."

They were quiet the next half-mile in the heavy traffic. People in other cars passing by in the slow traffic were glancing at the squad car, some pointing fingers of recognition. At first they stared incomprehensively, then they smiled with recognition and waved at the hero. Julian didn't acknowledge, he didn't really see what was going on. He was only thinking.

"I have another request," said Julian. "I'd like to see Barbara. Is that possible - right now?"

Brown smiled slightly, lifted his mike from its holder. "HQ, this is Brown, my 1020 will be Baptist Memorial hospital for about the next hour. Out."

"10-4."

As they neared the hospital the radio crackled again. "Lieutenant Brown, we have some interesting news concerning Julian's case."

Brown and Julian glanced at each other quizzically.

"This is Brown. Go ahead, HQ."

"During our research on Julian our **Family Tree** program spit out some interesting information." There was a hint of humor in the dispatcher's voice.

A pregnant pause as Brown pulled into the Hospital parking lot and drove to an emergency vehicle space at the front door.

"It seems that Professor Dawson is a distant cousin of Julian on his mother's side."

Julian and Brown looked at each other, stunned.

"No shit?" mumbled Julian and Brown at the same time.

*Barbara, this is Julian,* signed Karen.

While Brown, the nurse, the officer on duty, and the specialist looked on, the two people at first looked at each other, not knowing exactly how to proceed. Then tears welling in her eyes, Barbara reached out both hands. Julian moved forward and they hugged each other lightly to avoid injuring her wound. He stepped back and looked her over, looking for the damage.

Barbara pulled her top up enough to reveal the bandage and smiled. He gently touched the bandage and smiled back.

"Why don't we let these two people have a moment alone," noted Brown.

"You've got fifteen minutes," said nurse Remington, winking.

Everyone left the room except Julian and the survivor.

"Can you read lips?"

Barbara nodded, and slowly made words with her lips but without making a sound. *If you speak very slowly.* She smiled again. Then said, "Thank you, Julian Barrin, for possibly saving my life." There were guttural noises with the last sentence, her emotions causing her heavy breathing to oscillate her throat and mouth.

"You're welcome," said Julian softly.

They talked a moment and she revealed that she hadn't known that she was shot, she just started bleeding. All the excitement had caused her senses to shut down, put her in a protective physiological cocoon. The bleeding had caused her to go into shock. She remembered Julian trying to help, but she was too incapacitated to respond coherently.

A strange look came over her and she mouthed, *Don't worry. It's not what you think.*

Julian looked puzzled. "What?"

Barbara smiled and slowly mouthed, *I...don't know why, I just felt like telling you that. Weird, huh?*

Julian's eyes widened as his head dipped in surprise. Then, he shook his head, staring at her in thought, remembering the strange morning in his attic. "No, not weird at all."

The people returned to the room and Brown informed Julian that he needed to leave. "Are you ready?"

Julian hated to leave, but nurse Remington smiled and held the door open. "I guess so." He leaned forward and gave Barbara another hug.

*Come back and see me.*

"I will," said Julian, smiling.


*3AM Barrin Residence*


Julian was standing in the middle of the restaurant with flames pouring in, threatening to devour him, while Bob Day reported in slow motion, his mouth hardly moving, and the cameraman simply watched and captured the event on tape. People were outside pounding on the walls of McDonald's. The pounding came much closer, much louder.

Julian sat up, sweating. "What a nightmare."

The pounding continued.

Someone was at the door. He looked at the bedside clock. "Who the hell?"

He cautiously opened his bedroom door on the first floor and peered out into the hallway. The pounding was growing louder and more frequent. "Julian." A man's voice. "It's Yellow Cab."

Julian froze in his tracks, wondering what the hell anyone would be here in a Yellow cab for at three in the morning. Finally, he rushed and peered through a curtain. He couldn't believe what he saw. He hurried to the door and lifted the securing chain, flicked the lock, and threw open the door.

"Julian. I received a call from an orderly at the hospital who told me that this young lady would be waiting at a back exit. I thought about calling the police and then I remembered the name, and of course your name. You're a fucking hero... pardon, oh well, she can't hear. Anyway, you're a hero and I figured the least I could do. So here she is." He looked at Barbara, held his hands up in a 'what should I do' gesture.

She gently nudged him back toward his taxi, mouthing *It's okay.*

Barbara then turned and walked toward Julian who, still in midnight shock and still coming out of a nightmare, finally came to his senses and walked her back into his living room. He was elated to see her, but his emotions were running away again. He was very confused. Why was she here? She was supposed to be recovering from a gunshot wound, though the bullet had passed through, she had lost a lot of blood.

He sat her down and asked slowly, What are you doing here?

She motioned to the hallway and stood carefully, still feeling some pain, and smiled while gently leading him down the hallway. Julian was totally perplexed. At first he had the craziest notion that she wanted to go to the bedroom, but she didn't pause at the bedroom door, she carefully walked up the stairs with his help, meanwhile, he was shaking his head at the mystery of it all.

Barbara stopped where the rope was secured to the wall. The GC men had placed it back exactly as they had found it.

She lifted the rope from its retainer and handed it to Julian.

He took the rope in a stupor, staring at her strange appearance, not actually realizing he had it in his hand.

Finally, he looked at the white rope as though seeing it for the first time. Then he realized, though he couldn't believe it, that she wanted him to pull the ceiling ladder down. "How?" He looked at her, put his eyes directly in front of hers. "How did you even know? Have you been here before?"

She shook her head.

"So how?"

She gently tugged on the rope in his hand. *I will explain*, she mouthed, and pointed, *up there*.

Julian, finally comprehending pulled on the rope, dropped the ladder and extended it fully, flush on the floor.

She placed a foot on the first rung and started her climb, slowly and carefully, with Julian in tow, hanging onto her thighs gently. He liked what he felt, he couldn't deny. He liked her. But this was not the time for those thoughts. He was dumbfounded that she was here in the first place, and he was totally confused that they were climbing together into his sacred space in the attic.

She finally reached the top and waited for him to help her work her way toward the center, then the other end of the attic. They walked carefully along the heavy wooden struts. It was dark, so he flicked on a light.

The first thing Julian noticed was that the locker shined from the far corner, beckoning as usual. But what was Barbara doing here and how did she know? Or did she know? He decided to wait and see what she was going to do.

She moved immediately toward the locker, and stood directly next to it, looking at the latch.

Julian watched her carefully sit down in front of the locker in the very space that he had occupied for maybe an hour each of the ten years during his personal ritual. She placed her hands on top of it. She was now a part of his sanctuary, joining his ritual. How, and why, he couldn't comprehend, but she was. Her eyes closed. She sat, silent for a moment; the serenity in her face was like a magnet, drawing Julian toward her.

She was nodding. He was even more incredulous. He finally realized what was happening. She was hearing them too. How. How in the world had she come upon this mystery? How could she possibly have been pulled into his world? He had thought all this time his world was one of make believe - insane even. His own imagination or insanity driving this bizarreness for ten years. But she was a living testimony something was happening here. Now. At this very moment.

She beckoned for Julian to join her. He carefully worked his way next to her and sat very close, Indian style. She placed her hand on his. Her eyes were closed again. For a moment, Julian wasn't certain what was happening, whether he was a bystander or a participant.

Then he heard the voices. The very voices he had doubted really existed. He looked at her. Her face was serene and then he heard something that totally startled him. *You aren't going crazy Julian. You've been communicating with your ancestors.*

Julian was amazed. He was hearing Barbara's voice. He could see something in her face that emulated a spiritual reckoning, is the best he could describe it. Her voice was beautiful. Then he heard them.

*We haven't been able to completely get through to you because you didn't believe. You were blocking us with your doubts; the energy was lost looking for but not completely finding your consciousness.*

Julian couldn't believe his ears, or his mind. He placed his free hand on the locker. It was like turning up the volume.

*Julian, you aren't going insane. Insanity, in your case isn't going to be hereditary. You did inherit my looks, but not my brother's cerebral neurosis. I too studied psychology and for the same reasons you've been studying. Curiosity and fear.*

*You should destroy the documents in this locker. They do no one any justice. They will only remind those who read them that many people in our family suffered a living nightmare.*

*This will be my final contact with you. Barbara is a beautiful soul. She cares a lot for you. She thanks you with all her heart that you were able to save her and come into her life.*

*You will learn one final truth today that will be very difficult to grasp. Trust Barbara. She will help you through this crisis.*

"But what-"

*Goodbye Julian.*

*6:05AM The Barrin Residence*

Julian left the living room couch, walked down the hall and found the bedroom door ajar. He found Barbara sleeping peacefully but the moment he laid eyes on her, her eyes popped open. She smiled.

"Good morning." He walked over to her side. "Did we dream all of that last night?"

She shook her head.

She mouthed *No, Julian, it was real. And what they said was true.*

"Why can't I hear your voice anymore?"

*That was a temporary gift from your ancestors. I'm afraid that's the last time you'll get to hear my voice.*

"I was afraid of that. I thought about it the rest of the night and came to that conclusion. I just hoped I was wrong."

A few minutes later they were in the kitchen fixing breakfast.

"We probably need to call the hospital and tell them where you are."

*It's okay, I left a note explaining where I was going,* she wrote to Julian on a sheet of paper she found on the kitchen counter.

"How are you feeling? Pretty sore?"

She quit writing and began enunciating very slowly with her lips. *No, I'm actually feeling very good. You wouldn't believe how fast I'm healing. Maybe your locker and your ancestors have something to do with that too.*

She peeled her bandage back. Julian couldn't believe his eyes. The redness was still there, but the wound looked like it was two weeks old. It was almost completely healed.

"What did he mean last night about a very difficult truth?"

She looked at him for a long time, her face bearing an unusual sadness. It scared Julian.

"What? What aren't you telling me?"

She deferred to the writing tablet again and started scribbling as fast as she could write.

*Don't worry, Julian, I'll be beside you. We'll face it together. Just like we did yesterday.* She smiled. He liked her smile. She was very pretty when she wasn't in pain and didn't have blood splattered all over her, and when she wasn't afraid. That seemed like so long ago.

*Remember what he said, Trust me,* she wrote. She squeezed his hand.

*The main thing is that you are okay, Julian. You aren't destined to become what your ancestor was. You will do well. You will learn a lot about the mind. You will become an expert.*

"How do you know?" said Julian, his teeth showing in a happy smile.

*Trust me.* She smiled and winked.

The phone rang.

Julian looked at Barbara. "That's probably the lieutenant. He's supposed to call and tell me the name." She was already nodding and smiling. She knew. How? But after last night, he no longer doubted anything being possible.

He snatched the receiver from the hook. "Hello," said Julian with unusual confidence.

"This is Lieutenant Brown, Julian. How are you feeling today? I understand you have company. How's your guest, Barbara?"

"Much better than yesterday, both of us."

"I can imagine. That's great."

Julian watched Barbara's face as he listened to Brown. There was no other way to describe what she was displaying. A quiet resolve. For what? What was she preparing for?

"Uh, Julian, we need you to come to the morgue and make an identification if you would. Could you do that in the next half hour?"

"At the morgue. Identification," repeated Julian, perplexed, a strange feeling suddenly coming over him. "What about the guy I...what about him? You said you would tell me who he was," said Julian, anxiety creeping into his voice.

Barbara was nodding slightly, smiling. Letting Julian know that this was something related to last night's message. The promise of his ancestor that he looked like so much. He would not inherit the cerebral genetics at least, thank God. That he would never forget.

"That's right, I did. You'll probably understand after you get here. I'll be waiting for you."

"Sure. Thanks Lieutenant," said Julian, not liking the queasy feeling in his stomach. He sat back on the sofa, his emotions again in a nervous jumble. Yesterday he had felt every emotion possible. Today he felt elation at Barbara's sudden appearance into his life. Now, mixed feelings of trepidation and sadness.

But why didn't he feel anger? He wondered. According to the psychologists, you're supposed to go through all the emotions including anger after the trauma he had experienced. But, he hadn't felt any anger yet. Just remorse and an occasional fear. Would he ever hear the voices again, he suddenly wondered? Quieting his mind, he realized they needed to get going.

Brown was waiting at the morgue, of all places. Julian did not want to go there first thing this morning. This was not his idea of a good way to start a morning. He just wanted to know the identity of the man he shot. Well, at least he wasn't being held at bay in a restaurant full of bodies - right, he suddenly thought of the irony-- now I'll be in a morgue -- full of bodies. Jeez.

Driving toward the morgue in downtown Little Rock, he wanted to think about Barbara who was sitting beside him. He didn't want to think anymore about the man who had killed so many, almost killing Barbara-- the man he finally had to kill. That sounded so weird. He had to kill. My God. He didn't want to think about the morgue. Why the hell did Brown think he needed to come to the morgue? It was unsettling. Barbara squeezed his hand. She knew, Julian was thinking. She already knows what I'm about to learn. What the hell could be so bad after yesterday?

*6:35AM Coroner's Office*

At the coroner's office, the smell was just like the movies and novels describe. Terrible. Medicinal, but not like cough syrup, not that pleasant, but something that you wouldn't take internally and live to talk about.

Lieutenant Brown was waiting in the lobby, in full uniform, gun hanging at his side, but not drawn like yesterday. He shook hands with Julian, and gave Barbara a gentle hug. "How are you feeling, honey?"

Barbara and Julian glanced at each other and winked. *Very well. I'm healing fast.*

"What in the world possessed you to take off like that? I mean, you can if you want, it was just so unexpected. You just being - well, shot, healing, and all. You're an amazing lady," said Brown.

Julian eyed Barbara with an If-you-only-knew look.

"Hope you're taking care of this guy," said Brown playfully. Barbara smiled broadly, nodding. Neither Brown nor Julian saw the smile immediately disappear when they turned to walk toward the area no one wants to visit in his lifetime.

"So, what's this all about, Lieutenant?"

Brown glanced down at Julian, and briefly at Barbara who smiled quietly. He was amazed at Barbara's composure after yesterday.

"Well, Julian, we learned quite a surprise yesterday when the GC unit went through the locker in your attic."

Julian almost fell over. "You went through the locker?"

"Oh yeah. We searched every square inch of your house, trying to find answers, trying to uncover anything about you that might give us a clue as to who you really were. We couldn't be sure you weren't some weirdo who was going to wig out on us when we least expected it. It's standard procedure under violent circumstances."

Julian was still shaking when they approached the door marked 'Lockers.' This is where the faint-of-heart don't belong, unless they're here for the worst possible reason: Identification, thought Julian. So, why the hell was he here?

"Julian I told you yesterday we couldn't tell you anything until we notified the next of kin. Well, I had a reason for that. You had just gone through some pretty bad moments and we didn't think it would be in anyone's best interest to spring such a big surprise on you. That's all I should probably say right now."

Julian looked at Barbara who looked back at him, squeezing his hands ever so hard, letting him know she was there. He couldn't imagine what these two knew that would be so devastating to him. Brown of course, didn't know that Barbara was aware of anything.

Julian's heart started pounding from the suspense that was building up by the seconds being the only one in the room who was in the dark. What was he about to discover that could be worse than what happened yesterday? Who did Brown want him to identify, for Christ's sake?

They stopped in front of a locker labeled simply with a temporary, taped on white 'B.' The room was suddenly quite chilly. Julian shuddered. Barbara leaned in close to him. They had just met less than twenty-four hours ago and she was the support of his life at this moment.

An attendant in a white lab coat approached and Brown nodded.

The man reached for the horizontal chrome handle, pulling deftly causing the gurney to slide gently but forcefully out in plain view. The body that inhabited this locker was covered with a heavy white sheet. The form, undeniably human, was quite dead. It would have frozen to death if it weren't already dead, he thought, wondering why he would have such a flippant thought. That's the way the mind works, he reminded himself. Comic relief, protection of the soul. Enough, get on with this thing. He was shaking from cold and suspense, not to mention the fear of what or who was under the sheet they all stared at.

"Julian, this is the man you shot yesterday in self defense."

Julian's eyes were wide with absolute surprise. Why would he have to suffer through this again? Seeing the man who turned his life upside down yesterday. Who almost killed him, and because of bizarre circumstances, almost got him killed again after the man's own death, because he, Julian, was at the wrong place at the wrong time.

"There is a slight change since you saw him last. His beard has been shaved."

Julian's thought since he first saw and was tempted to remove the wallet in the man's back pocket in McDonald's: I shot this man. *What is his name?*

Enduring incredible suspense, Julian thought his heart would jump from his body until they pulled the sheet back. When the sheet was finally pulled to the waist by the attendant, Julian stared absently for a long moment. Not sure what to think. Is this what Brown wanted him to see? There was a puncture wound where the bullet had entered the body. The puncture wound that Julian had caused using this once-alive man's own gun.

The attendant left them to their own devices, delighted to leave the frigid room.

The face and the body didn't sink in for a long moment. Yes, he looked different because he didn't have a beard. But something wasn't clicking in Julian. Maybe because he was so cold, his mind wasn't cataloging as it normally would. He was covered in goose bumps; such a chilling end to 10 years of doubt. He thought about the attic and how that haunted world had finally ended on a happy note. 10 years! Of doubt. He didn't have to worry anymore. He even thought about Professor Dawson for a split second, and his strange but supportive behavior through it all. Julian kept staring at the cold body. Did he think it would talk to him like those in the attic? What a chilling ridiculous idea. Those in the attic were good spirits. This man was a tortured soul. Brown and Barbara were alternating their attention between Julian and the body. Barbara's gaze finally settled on Julian with incredible empathy. Brown glanced at the bullet hole, then, he pulled the sheet up to cover all but the neck and the face. The bullet hole was no longer visible. But Julian would always see that bullet hole. It was imprinted on his brain for the rest of his natural life.

"What?" whispered Julian in exasperation, still wondering why he was here with all these dead people. *Where is his family? Why aren't they here freezing their asses off?*

He'd just about had enough of this. Jeez. Mental charade.

*Patience!* Was that them or me? No way. That part is behind me. They're gone. Julian kept staring at the face; aware of Barbara and the Lieutenant who stood by expectantly wondering when the puzzle would sink in. Wait. Something clicked. His mind was finally beginning to assimilate.

*Wait a minute. What is his name?*

"What is his name?" Julian whispered, staring at the body.

Blond hair. Same color as Julian's.

Brown did something that surprised even Barbara. Brown reached down and carefully rolled both eyelids back.

Julian was too involved, too stunned with the whole thing

that morning, to react or feel anything. He just kept observing and waiting for the big moment, the revelation he was warned about. While the Lieutenant held the lids back, Julian practically held his breath and quietly gazed realizing this act was supposed to be significant. *What? I've had enough dead people to last a lifetime!*

Blue eyes staring at eternity. Same blue as Julian's. He'd seen them in a mirror that very morning.

Nose. Nice nose. Like Julian's. Lips. Full, like Julian's.

Julian changed positions, letting Barbara's hand go loose; he walked to the other side and peered down, then pulled back. Sizing up what he was seeing. Brown and Barbara waited ever so patiently.

Lips pursed, Julian realized something was starting to sink in. He knew this man. Not just from yesterday either. He knew this man from somewhere way back there. This man so familiar - so sudden, that it startled Julian. He leaned back and turned to look at the letter on the door. The white tape with B on it.

It couldn't be. This was the terrible truth that Julian was going to learn. But this couldn't be. This man was never supposed to become a man. This man died as a young child, a baby. So he was told.

In shock, Julian leaned against the cold locker; the sticky freezing touch didn't even faze him. He finally comprehended what everyone else already knew. He was about to collapse from the revelation when Barbara suddenly appeared at his side and gave support.

"My God! I don't believe this!" He shouted. His eyes were glazing over. Barbara put her arms around his waist, offering as much support as he would allow. "No," he started sobbing, shaking his head in vehement denial. Tears were streaming down his cheeks. Brown pulled the cover back over the face and shoved the gurney back to its resting position deep inside a cold oblivious ending. Infinity -- beyond man's comprehension.

A kaleidoscope of cerebral colors blinded Julian for an instant as his memory jump started back to his early childhood. *It takes many strange things to bring the traumatized memory to the surface at times.* Professor Dawson. Julian remembered taking a bath with a three-year-old named Kevin. And having his head pushed under water and hearing Kevin laughing, like it was a game. While he was swallowing bath water, he could clearly see the cruel smile above the water. He had almost drowned. They came in and pulled Kevin off. Then he never saw that face again. Julian had been traumatized and lost his memory. He didn't remember anything from the time he was born up to and including that moment in the tub. Until today.

*Your brother died at birth, Julian.*

"I killed my own twin brother," he whispered so low that only the acoustics that belonged to the cold and the dead caused everyone to hear.

# Final Moment

The morgue was like the North Pole, a white room of blinding lights so there was no Shift like the morning sun in the attic. But there was Shadow Play. Julian heard a rustling somewhere in the cold room of the dead behind thick stainless steel doors. No one else appeared to notice. Barbara and the lieutenant were casual observers simply biding their time until Julian completed his moment in this cold sanctuary for the dead.

Then the lights went out! It was pitch dark. No one moved. No one breathed.

Then there was faint light. Julian smelled a familiar odor. Not formaldehyde. He smelled Christmas ornaments. And he was back in his attic. The locker was sitting in front of him. He remembered something he forgot to do. Kevin, the ghost, had said, Destroy these documents. Julian hurriedly opened the locker and grabbed the journal that he had read for 10 years. He imagined the intruder while he performed his final act in this attic. The intruder who had ripped out the page. Julian began ripping the journal into shreds...he closed the chest without returning the journal. He kept the pieces and started to head back to the ladder. Then there was Shadow Play and the skeleton danced. There were no eyes but they were looking straight at Julian.

"*I'm not gone yet. As you know, we ghosts have a long memory!*"

Julian found himself back in the morgue. His hands were empty.

"Just when I thought I was sane."

Printed in the United States
204071BV00002B/169-216/P